ABOUT THIS BOOK

THE LOST STAR
by H. M. Hoover

The routine supply run had become anything but routine. After crash-landing her air car, Lian Webster wondered if she would make it back to her parents' observatory on time—or if they would even miss her. But when a member of Balthor's archaeological team rescues her and offers her a chance to remain on the site, Lian finds that she can't refuse. The moment she walked onto the scene of the puzzling excavation, Lian felt that something was compelling her to stay. Ignoring her work as an astrophysicist, Lian set out to explore the area, and the strange, fearless creatures who populated the camp. The lumpies, gray-furred creatures with strange, expressionless eyes, were everywhere. Gentle and seemingly unintelligent, they appeared to be reaching out to her. The lumpies had a secret, and when Lian discovered it, she knew that life on Balthor would never be the same.

OTHER BOOKS BY H. M. HOOVER

The Delikon

The Rains of Eridan

This Time of Darkness

The Lost Star

H. M. Hoover

Puffin Books

PUFFIN BOOKS

Viking Penguin Inc., 40 West 23rd Street, New York, New York 10010, U.S.A.
Penguin Books Ltd, Harmondsworth, Middlesex, England
Penguin Books Australia Ltd, Ringwood, Victoria, Australia
Penguin Books Canada Limited, 2801 John Street, Markham, Ontario, Canada L3R 1B4
Penguin Books (N.Z.) Ltd, 182–190 Wairau Road, Auckland 10, New Zealand

First published by Viking Penguin Inc. 1979
Published in Puffin Books 1986
Copyright © H. M. Hoover, 1979
All rights reserved
Printed in U.S.A. by Offset Paperback Mfrs., Inc., Dallas, Pennsylvania
Set in Electra

Library of Congress Cataloging in Publication Data
Hoover, H. M.   The lost star.
Reprint. Originally published: New York: Viking Penguin, 1979.
Summary: While on an archaeological expedition to Balthor,
a young astrophysicist stumbles upon the Lumpies,
gray smiling creatures with a strange secret.
[1. Science fiction]   I. Title.
[PZ7.H7705Lo   1986]   [Fic]   86-4881   ISBN 0-14-032166-7

To
Rosie

The Lost Star

PROLOGUE

Long ago, when their star aged and burned so that the ninth planet withered and its seas grew hot, the people fled their world. The network of Counters told them when and where and how, and their orbiting ships streamed out into the dark of space. Their bright star, forgotten, swelled upon itself and began to shed its fiery mass into the stellar winds.

On other worlds, where life went on, the dying star was seen. Some had evolved enough to grunt at it in wonder, others sang to celebrate its beauty, some made up myths of supernatural happenings, and a few, a very few, analyzed its nuclear reactions. All were ignorant of its doomed planets.

The Counters calculated and scattered the ships, the life containers, as our wind scatters maple keys, and like those winged seeds, only a small number remained viable until new suns gave them world and water and time. One Counter found a favorable world and a form of continuity for the life its own ship contained. That was long before Earth's people found and named that same world Balthor.

1

There was something dreadful out there in the dark; she was sure of that. Just as sure as she had been at the age of four, when something terrible lurked beneath her bed and she knew that if she put a toe over the edge, it would grab her foot. At four, she would lie rigid with fear until sleep freed her. Now she was fifteen and alone in the night of another world; sleep would not come, and she was trapped not by her imagination but by the wreckage of her aircar.

She had gone to Limai spaceport to pick up a load of supplies—a routine trip. On the way home a storm had overtaken her freight-laden craft. Tornado winds lifted her to heights no sane pilot would attempt, spun her across the sky, and left her to drop through dark clouds where lightning lurked and struck this small interloper as it fell.

All electrical equipment, all computerized instruments went dead. She fought with the few manual controls to right the craft, to pull it up, and suddenly saw row on row of mountains jutting up below. Hailstones racketed against the windows. When the crash came, it was in rain so dense she could not see. The craft belly-landed, skimming over treetops like a stone skipped across waves. The last thing she heard was the banshee scream of branches against the metal hull.

It was night when she woke, surprised to find herself alive. Her body was slumped in the pilot's seat behind the safety mesh; her head lolled painfully to the side. There was the salty taste of blood in her mouth, and her lips and tongue felt swollen, as if she had bitten them or smashed against something. She was so disoriented and it was so dark that it took her some time to make sure she wasn't badly hurt. She had no idea where she was, and she was frightened.

Wanting to get out, without thinking what might be out there, she freed herself from the mesh. The hatch wouldn't open, either by button or by manual trip-bar. There was a hole somewhere; she could feel a draft. A hole meant insects could get in. At the thought her ankles began to itch; her neck felt as if something with many tiny legs were marching under her hair. She scratched vigorously and found no insects and no bites. How silly, her common sense reminded her, to narrowly miss death and then worry about insects. She took a deep breath to relax and leaned back against the seat. Thoughtless panic would never do.

The rain stopped. Through the window she could see trees, black against a jagged dark horizon. Insects sang. From the distance came a rhythmic *tock-tock* sound. There were birdlike trills, high-pitched squeaks, soft songlike ululations, the small footsteps of forest creatures going about their business. The air smelled of wet humus and of plants crushed by her wreck.

The clouds were blowing away, and the stars seemed a reassuring link with home. She wasn't aware when the silence began; she only noticed when, one by one, the sounds outside ceased. When the last insect stopped singing, the trees sighed in a sudden wind. For no reason she shivered, and goose bumps rose on her arms. Something was out there.

A heavy branch snapped. There was a loud sniff, then a second, clearer and more distinct, as if a head had turned in her direction. Twigs cracked and broke against a moving bulk or bulks. Grass rustled. The wreckage shuddered slightly, as if touched against its will.

Lian curled down in her seat to get below window level. If it could hunt in the dark, it had night vision. She could not see it—but it could see her. She had been told by experts that the carnivores of Balthor could not feed on foreign protein; it made them very ill. Now she wondered, Had the carnivores been told?

Something heavy stepped onto the wing, stood there, ponderously walked forward, paused, and then began to try to force open the windows. Lian bit her lip to keep from crying out, and slid down into the space between the pilot's seat and the control panel. The floor was wet and gritty; broken wires jabbed her. For a moment she worried that the wires might be hot, then forgot about it as the wreck abruptly tilted; a heavy body lurched against the pilot's dome and fell to the ground with a cry.

As if in anger, the thing pounded on the wing until all the metal warbled. Plastic fragments from the dome rained on her head. There was a second drumming, less vigorous, and weird moaning sounds. The wreckage gave a final bounce and was still.

She was afraid to move. Her knees ached from crouching in this awkward nook; a sharp fragment was poking her thigh. She rested her forehead against the seat and was aware of being very tired. She thought of her own bed; it seemed the most desirable thing in the world.

Home was somewhere out there in the darkness of this nearly empty planet, on a high, bleak plateau beneath seven large white domes. Inside each dome enormous telescopes silently wheeled and turned, staring up at the stars, observing, recording, evaluating the formation and evolution of this unknown portion of the universe. And all to satisfy the infinite curiosity of humans.

Lian knew that while the two astrophysicists who were her parents could comfortably envision the creation and death of the Milky Way, they would probably not notice her failure to show up for dinner.

Which might be just as well; no sense worrying them. The computer would have followed her flight as long as power lasted in her ship. The observatory's orbiting satellite would have tracked her the rest of the way. They would find her in the morning.

A night creature gave a tentative call. Another answered. Insects began to sing, hesitantly at first, then with renewed confidence. The danger had gone.

Very quietly Lian pulled herself up onto the seat and brushed herself off. This was not the best of beds, but it would do. She had almost drifted off to sleep when from the distance came a long, mournful cry. The night chorus paused to listen and be reassured, then resumed louder than before.

But the cry echoed in Lian's mind and banished sleep. It was as if she had heard herself cry out with an old fear of being lost and alone. In a sense, she thought, she had been ever since she was eight and left Earth with her parents. The fears had been buried, as feelings usually were, but they were still with her here in the dark.

She had never admitted that to herself before, how lonely she had been as a child among adults . . . adults who were well-meaning and correct, but bored by a child and preoccupied with their own work and passions.

Because of the nomadic nature of her parents' profession, they had had the choice of leaving her in school on Earth and possibly never seeing her again, or taking her with them to space colonies, to other worlds, to always remote outposts. Her playmates had been few and far between. Her teachers were computers, but she had had access to any advanced education she chose. She had chosen astronomy; at least some of the astronomy teachers were human, members of her parents' staff. She liked the subject and studied hard and well. There were few distractions.

When she was fourteen, her first simple paper was published, "Spectrographic Analysis of the Titanium Composition of A-62.83-3.3 as a Feasible Ore Source." At fifteen a comet bore her name. Less than a month before, she had proudly become the youngest salaried member of the observatory staff. Her parents were pleased. Not so all the staff. Some muttered "nepotism"; others watched this slender, dark-haired girl pass them in the hall, so intent, so serious, and asked her if she was happy, as if they thought she wasn't. It had bothered her before. Now, as she thought about them, their opinions seemed unimportant.

It was a very long night. Several times she dozed off, and then her dreams would review those last few conscious seconds before the crash, and she would jerk awake, heart pounding. An hour before dawn the adrenalin was exhausted and she went limp in dreamless sleep.

A herd of nalas woke her as they grazed around the wreck. Like green-and-white-striped goats, they bleated out comments on the morning. The sun was almost up. That cheered her; help would be here soon. She pressed the emergency beacon button. It was still dead.

Sitting up, she saw that her aircar had slid off the canopy of trees, slewed left, and plowed halfway across a meadow. The skid marks were a wavering brown scar against the green.

Movement caught her eye. In the furrow behind her a flock of blue-crested bidernecks swooped down on a hapless lizard. They swarmed up from a skeleton, these avian piranhas, to circle and light upon the tailfin of the aircar. The scent of something trapped inside excited them to chirps and screeches. Not yet birds but no longer reptiles, bidernecks were scavengers and very good at their job.

Lian turned to watch them. At her first move they framed the window like gargoyles. She shrank back against the seat. Beady-eyed, clinging with claw-tipped wings, they were six inches high and black. With their horse heads and long teeth, they appeared to be constantly smiling a terrible smile.

There was a scratching noise behind her. A biderneck was trying to force its way through a crack in the window. She poked at it. The biderneck promptly bit her finger. But even as it did so, an expression of revulsion came over the creature. It scrambled back, chittering frantically, wiping its teeth on the pane, on other bidernecks, on anything it could. It made spitting sounds, as if it had tasted something disgusting. There was a flurry of sniffing and chitters, and the flock abruptly took wing.

She couldn't stand being trapped in here a minute longer. If the hatch would not open, maybe the dome would. She got up on the seat. It was too cramped for her to stand erect, so she pushed from a stooped position, first with both hands, then with her shoulders. The dome creaked but would not release.

The effort did, however, produce a sharp headache. When she touched the side of her face where the worst pain was, she discovered a lump and tenderness. "A black eye," she said, and went back to shoving and wincing.

Boink! The seat beneath her feet rocked left. She grabbed at the ceiling to keep from falling. The hatch had sprung open, ramp down, its weight tilting the entire wreck.

Lian stepped out onto the wing and looked around. To be outdoors at the Mount Balthor Observatory was to see a world of mountaintops and sky, bare rock and snow, clouds and wind. Sometimes it had seemed to her that Balthor was as desolate as the stars. Limai spaceport hardly counted. It was like all terminals, shabby and impersonal, full of aliens en route to other places. But this mountain valley with encircling wooded hills, sweet grass, animals, and gentle breeze had the coziness of Earth.

Well, perhaps not quite, she thought, remembering the creature who had terrified her the night before, and wondering where it was at the moment, and what it was.

She sat down on the crumpled tail section. It was cold and wet with dew, and she slid to the ground. Rainwater trapped in a wing hollow reminded her she was both thirsty and hungry. Her last meal had been yesterday's lunch. She cupped some water in her hand, took a sip, and spit it out. It tasted of dust, metallic residue, and a bitterness she couldn't define. A green birdlike creature, attracted by the flash of water, landed beside her, bent down to drink, and also spit. It looked up at her and cocked its head questioningly.

"I'm waiting to be rescued," she told it, and then winced as her lip pulled in speech. The bird did not seem sympathetic and quickly flew off. The nala herd wandered away down the clearing, and she was alone again.

It was perhaps ten o'clock in the morning when the hum of a motor became audible between bird songs. The hills created an echo; it was impossible to tell from which direction the sound came. As she turned, the sun mirror-flashed off something in the west. She squinted to see. Some sort of alien craft was approaching.

The strange craft circled and recircled the clearing, blowing the grass flat with its jets, whipping leaves and dust high in the air. Lian turned her back and closed her eyes against debris. She heard rather than saw the craft set down. There was a hissing sigh as the motor shut off. A hatch spring sang out. Brushing her hair back from her face, she turned and saw a man running toward her, a stranger.

2

He was tall, brown skinned, and gaunt. His curly white hair gleamed in the sun, but he appeared younger than her father. He was dressed in tan clothes and work boots, and tools jangled from his belt.

"Are you all right?" he called. His accent was cultured and of Earth. Now that she could see him clearly, she relaxed somewhat. His face was kind if not handsome, his expression a mixture of concern and puzzlement. "Should you be walking about? You look rather pale." As he came up to her, he reached out and gently but firmly touched her chin and turned her bruised face to the light. "Is that very painful?" he asked, frankly studying her.

"It's fine," she said, wondering who he was. "I'm always pale. It comes from studying at night and sleeping days." She took a step back. "I'm very glad to see you. Who are you?"

"A reasonable question," the man said and smiled. "Jeffrey Farr." He nodded toward his aircraft. "As you probably guessed by the flags, we're here on a field trip."

Lian had not noticed the insignia. It was painted on the open hatch and identified the craft as belonging to the "Balthor Archaeological Research Expedition, Interstellar Geographic Society and Central Pacific University, Joint Sponsors. Dr. J. Farr, Comm."

"What are archaeologists doing on Balthor? I thought this was a Class Five planet. There's no civilization—is there?"

"No more," the man agreed, "but there was once. We don't know yet if it was native or if the planet served as a colony for another world, but habitations do exist. Now, if you will forgive my curiosity, who are you?"

She stared at him. "Lian Webster, of course. Who were you searching for?"

He suppressed a smile. "No one—living."

Lian felt herself blush with confusion. "You didn't know I was here?"

"No," the man said. "I was site-hunting. I saw the sun glinting off your aircraft, wondered what it was, and flew over to check. Are you alone?"

"Yes—I crashed last night—"

"Good Lord! Lian Webster, where are you from?"

"Mount Balthor Observatory."

"That's a thousand miles away at least! How did you end up here? We must call them at once." His obvious concern was somehow very comforting.

She told him and then looked down at her white pants and jacket. They were dirt-stained and spotted with blood from her split lip. "Do I look very terrible? Will they be upset when they see me on the screen?"

"I imagine they're upset already, but your appearance won't be an added shock. There's no screen on my craft. Just a radio."

It took almost five minutes to get the observatory to respond to their call. When someone finally answered, it was Max, one of the maintenance crew. He seemed surprised to hear she was not in Limai. "We thought the storm grounded you," he said. "It's still raining there, and we've got heavy snow a mile below us."

Lian didn't really care about his weather report. "Can I speak with either of my parents?"

"Sorry. They're both in the big dome. They've got the no-admittance, no-calls rule in effect."

"This is an emergency, Max. You can interrupt."

"Look—uh—give me your channel code," he said, and then, to her extreme irritation, went off the air with, "I'll get back to you."

Nobody even noticed I was missing, she thought, but said aloud, "He's going to call back," which was unnecessary since Dr. Farr had heard the entire conversation.

"Yes." His tone was noncommittal, and he was staring off into space as if distracted by another thought. "Your parents are—" he started to say and then took a deep breath and changed his mind. "Are you hungry?"

"I'm starving," she said honestly. "I haven't eaten since lunchtime yesterday. And I'm very thirsty!"

"Good. I've just the thing."

As he rummaged about in a container under the bolted-in pilot's seat, she looked the craft over. "What kind of vehicle is this? I never saw one like it."

"Tolat truck. Great design, isn't it? It's a bit functional—but they don't need seats—here we go!" He handed her several food boxes.

Over the fruit drink and chocolate protein bars she told him the details of her adventure. He listened with his eyes, so closely that his own fleeting expressions registered any changes in her face. She sat on the open hatch, he cross-legged on the ground, totally at ease.

"It pounded on the wing?" he said. "In rage or pain?"

"I don't know—I was too scared to tell."

He nodded. "I would have been too." He looked over at her aircar and shook his head in wonder. "You're one fine pilot, Lian Webster!"

"I'm one lucky pilot," she said, and he grinned at her.

"That animal of yours bothers me a little," he said. "There aren't supposed to be dangerous animals of that size around here. According to the experts. I never trust experts in things like that." He stood up. "There's really no point waiting here. Your people can pick you up at our base far more conveniently than here."

"What about my aircar? It doesn't look like much now, but it's very expensive equipment."

"We'll call the wrecker at Limai. They can come pick it up with a magnetic hoist." He walked over to the wreck. "Do you want to salvage the supplies?"

"If we can."

While they were transferring cartons to the other ship, the radio beeper went on again. Dr. Farr was in the truck and took the call. It was very brief, and he seemed to spend most of the time listening. He came out with a bemused expression.

"That was Max," he said, and Lian frowned. "Would you—uh—like to join us on the dig? Be our guest?"

"If I could," she said politely, wondering why he was issuing an invitation now. "How long will you be on Balthor? You see, we're expecting a star to supernova any time now, and that's going to keep us all busy. It's very lucky—you don't often get to see the actual explosion. . . ." The expression on his face made her pause. "What is it?"

"Well, that's just it. Apparently the nova has occurred and no one . . . I suggested we fly you back to Limai and they could meet us there. . . ." He paused to choose the kindest words. "None of the observatory staff can be spared to pick you up at the moment. And I'm afraid our trucks can't brave the high mountains with the chance of running into a storm up there."

"Oh," said Lian, and suddenly she was very tired. But not surprised by the decision. It was quite like her parents. She appreciated Dr. Farr's tact but knew exactly what the reality was. They were in charge of the observatory. It was a choice between having their full staff recording a supernova as it happened or someone's missing part of that experience to come and get her. And since she was safe, after all, she could wait. They would have let anyone else wait. Her personal interest in the event was incidental. Their work came first. Tears burned her eyes, and she turned her back and blinked rapidly, not wanting a stranger to see. "How long until they—"

"At least a week."

"That's an imposition on you," she said. "I'm sorry."

"Not at all," he assured her. "It will be a pleasure to have you as our guest."

Lian said very little during the hour's ride to the archaeologists' base. She politely answered Dr. Farr's questions, but after several futile attempts to draw her into conversation her rescuer decided she was worn out from her ordeal and left her alone. But it wasn't fatigue that kept her silent. She was thinking, trying to decide if, in her parents' position, she could have done the same thing.

I can understand, she thought. They cannot make exceptions for me. But it seemed to her that, if the situation had been reversed, she would have hurried to them even if three stars went into supernova and formed a black hole on camera. Perhaps that was because she was young. They ascribed many of her "wrong" decisions to her youth. Perhaps, when she was their age, when she had spent so many years studying distant lights in the sky, her perspective of human affairs would have altered. But at the moment her feelings were hurt. She did *not* understand. She did not want to understand. She wanted to cry.

"That's our base there—on the bluff above the bend in the river," Dr. Farr announced. "If you look down the valley to the southeast, you'll see the outline of an old city."

The base was obvious, with its street of yellow-dome housing units and large white X-mark landing pad. All she could see in the forest to the southeast was a series of large wooded mounds. Only slowly did she realize the mounds formed a pattern of a great green eye. A red dirt road led from the camp to the corner of the eye, like a tear's trace.

As she looked down on it, a curious murmur filled her mind, like a song remembered in a dream. She could almost understand the words, as if she had once known what they meant. Then it stopped.

She glanced over at Dr. Farr; he appeared unaffected. The phenomenon was probably the result of too many altitude and air pressure changes on her inner ears, she decided. Or perhaps the protein bar had disagreed with her.

In the ancient structure below, beneath the center of the eye, the Counter added One.

3

In the time between landing and late afternoon, Lian forgot her hallucination. Dr. Farr led her directly from the truck to the medical dome, where she spent a naked hour alone being analyzed and intimidated by the medicom's probings. When she emerged, she had had a medicated shower, a thorough physical, which found her tired and bruised but healthy, and her fill of that pushy machine's smug androgenous voice issuing orders.

She had often been told it was an immature trait—being irked by computers. Perhaps it was, but Lian secretly thought most machines developed personality traits of their own, and some were hostile to humans or felt superior. Which means I am probably paranoid as well as childish, she was thinking as she came out, combing her wet hair with her fingers.

Dr. Farr was waiting, sitting on his haunches on the path by the door. Seeing her expression, he stood up, concerned. "Everything O.K.?"

"Fine. Just cuts and bruises. And your medicom wants me to cut my hair to avoid contamination by mold spores."

"It tells us all that," he said with a grin. "I suspect it was programmed by a bald fanatic. Ignore it and come see where you'll be staying. I fixed up the guest module for you, and we moved in some clothes and toiletries, as Dr. Scott calls them. She's our language expert, Earthly and otherwise. She's a redhead and was born in the spring. Her parents named her Robin, but if you're wise, you'll call her Scotty. Let's get you some real food, and you can meet the staff when they come back for lunch . . . and I'll show you . . ." He chattered on so cheerfully and was so obviously glad to have her there that her spirits began to rise.

Of all the people she met at lunch, human and nonhuman, the only face she remembered was Dr. Scott's. Perhaps because the woman had eyes that crinkled into laughter at unexpected moments. Lian was at that stage of physical exhaustion where the mind functions on instinct; she could not have rationally explained why she liked Dr. Scott on first hello; she just did. Just as she disliked the staff photographer, whose name was Vincent. By the time lunch was over, she hadn't slept in thirty-six hours, and all she wanted to do was take a nap.

Her guest house resembled a small yellow igloo with two round windows and a vent pipe. Inside, a bath module made one wall flat. In contrast to the brilliant exterior, the interior was a restful beige, the furnishings spartan but adequate. The bed felt wonderfully soft. Luxuriating in the feel of it, she stretched and yawned and pushed a pillow under her left ear.

Dr. Farr and Dr. Scott had told her so much over lunch that it was hard to remember it all. There were some fifty staff members, about half of them human. There were five amalfi—lavender creatures with bodies like four tubular arms, bulbous heads, and purple beaks that spoke in rapid clicks. Highly intelligent, they came from a world wetter than Balthor. They suffered discomfort here and wore breathing-assist apparatuses but persisted because they sought evidence of a long-lost colony of their own. The balance of the staff were dwarf tolats. The tolats' names all sounded like interrupted snores. A race crablike in appearance, they were known for their engineering and mechanical talents, durability, and total lack of imagination. The airtruck was of tolat design, as was much of the equipment here.

She rather liked the assortment, the variety of the mix, Lian decided, thinking it over. At the observatory the staff was all human; there once had been several amalfi, but they had been unable to endure the dry cold of the mountains and of the human mind. She had never talked with a tolat, and she found them very alien. But that, no doubt, would change, she thought, and fell into a long, deep sleep.

She was dreaming of her grandmother's house on Earth; she could smell the grass and hear someone walking in the garden. Footsteps crunching on gravel, a gardener working. There was something special about today, she remembered, some glad reason to get up. She opened her eyes, saw the round room, and remembered. The dream slipped away—far back into the past. But part of the gladness stayed.

During the night someone had covered her with a green plaid blanket. It smelled faintly of sunshine and perfume, and she decided her benefactor was Dr. Scott. They are really very nice, she thought, to be so gracious to a total stranger. Her parents, faced with the same situation, would page someone like Max and give him responsibility for the guest. There would be no question of spending time so unproductively as to think of blankets. She checked her watch. They would be going to bed now at the observatory, or sitting in the dining room discussing the night's viewing, engrossed in radiant energy emitted from the exploded star . . . she was missing it all. . . . She got up and went in to shower and put on clean clothes. Half an hour later she walked out into the morning.

The trees around the camp dew-glistened in the sunlight. The river winked at the bottom of the bluff. What she called birds, for lack of knowing their proper names, perched upon the fronds, their morning songs mingled with the throbs of amphibians from the marsh somewhere below. Off in the distance other creatures could be heard. Lian had no idea what they were.

A few igloos down the street, Dr. Scott was mowing the long grass around a flowering shrub, manicuring raw nature into a lawn for her home. Lian watched for a moment and then began to laugh. Insects flew, hopped, or walked out of the path of the cutter bar. Large frog-mouthed birds, like unkempt bags of blue feathers, marched about, scooping up the insects. Each time the birds swallowed, they paused in their walk; a look of almost insane gratification crossed their owlish faces; their amber eyes closed, and they gave a chesty cry of "Wortle!" Then, with a quick ruffle, they recovered their dignity and marched on.

Impulsively Lian knelt and picked up one of the birds; it was surprisingly heavy. Its feet went on walking on air as she held it. It regarded her with a direct stare, then quite audibly burped. She quickly set it down. It continued its walk as if nothing had happened.

"What are they?" she called to Dr. Scott.

"Wortles," came the answer. "They act like toy birds. Watch them —after a time you start looking for the key in their backs." Her next words were drowned out by three wortles at once. Lian started off down the path to join her.

A black beetle half the size of her hand darted out from beneath a clump of leaves, paused, then raced the other way and dodged into the tall grass. It was no sooner gone than a fuzzy orange millipede some two feet long and six inches in diameter flowed across the path. Feathery brown antennae quivered as it followed the route of the beetle. It all happened so quickly Lian didn't even have time to be upset.

As if this creature's appearance gave evidence of her ability to flush out game, two wortles came flopping over and landed on the path beside her. She stopped. "You go ahead," she invited them. They ignored her and to her delight marched sideways like demented sentries until she turned and proceeded. Then she saw that each visible staff member had its complement of wortles.

"I never knew there was so much wildlife down here," she said as the woman turned off the mower to talk. "I nearly got knocked down by a worm."

"Big orange one?" said Dr. Scott, and when Lian nodded, "That's Buford. He's the camp pet. He controls our black beetle population. He's tame but you must be careful when you pet him. He has an acid tongue."

"I'll—uh—watch out for it," said Lian. Having no intention of petting a worm, but not wanting to offend local tastes, she added, "He is . . . lovely. And very quick, too."

Dr. Scott laughed, delighted by Lian's attempt to be tactful. "You don't like him, do you? There's no accounting for tastes. How do you feel about lumpies?"

"I've never seen one. The cargo men at Limai call each other lumpies as if it were an insult. Are they animals?"

"The cargo men are, yes. I'm not sure about the lumpies." She paused. "Dr. Farr and the others say so. . . ."

"Are there lumpies around here?"

"Some. They live in the hills of the old city. One comes up here every morning to feed Buford."

Lian frowned. "The worm is their pet, too?"

"Maybe . . ." Dr. Scott obviously had never thought of that. "Maybe that's why Buford's been tame since the beginning . . . there he is."

Lian turned cautiously, expecting to see Buford. She saw instead a large gray creature walking on four legs. "What an odd-looking . . ." she started to say and then stopped, for the lumpie had paused in midstep at the sight of her. It stood erect, and they were at eye level.

The lumpie was not a beautiful animal. It was squat and heavy, with smooth pearl-gray skin. Unlike the other animals she had seen here, this one was a hexapod. Its mid and rear legs were short and stocky, and it could walk on four legs or stand erect on the wide-spaced rear feet with mid legs folded against its belly. Its "arms" were oddly jointed, and its hands many-fingered like a gray sea anemone. It was short-necked, its high-set ears petal-shaped. The roundness of its head made the wide mouth form a clownlike smile beneath a short seal muzzle.

For what seemed like minutes to Lian, they stared at each other in the shock of some sort of recognition. Now she was aware only of its eyes, blue with rims and striations of dark blue, eyes large enough to belong to a nocturnal creature, eyes that peered into her mind like some alien camera and let her see into a soul where such quiet joy danced that she smiled.

It seemed to Lian as she stared that it knew—knew her being here was no accident but a thing predestined, knew what she had been and was and would be—and approved.

"Lian?" Dr. Scott touched her arm. "Lian? Look at me!" A certain urgency in the voice made Lian obey, but regretfully. "They can almost hypnotize you. Please don't look or stare at them too long."

"What are they?" Lian was almost whispering. She saw Dr. Scott start to say something, then change her mind.

"Don't give them human feelings," she said. "They aren't . . . human. Possibly not even very intelligent. But gentle."

"Do they talk?"

"I've never heard one make any noise."

"Are they telepaths?"

"Do you think they are?"

Lian didn't know her well enough to judge if the woman was mocking her—but instinctively she felt not. "You *do* think they're telepaths!"

"But we're not, are we?" Dr. Scott said, and that seemed to sadden her. "Sometimes I wish . . ."

"What?"

"I wish they'd quit playing the fool!"

At the hint of anger in the woman's voice the lumpie dropped to four feet and approached, smiling its built-in smile. In one hand it carried a bulgy woven string bag. Dr. Scott looked at it, then shook her head in resignation and smiled at the creature. "Good morning, Billy," she said. The lumpie sat down on its haunches like an odd dog.

"You give them bags to collect things?" said Lian.

"No. They weave them from grass. They make hammocks for beds, too." She gave an unexpectedly piercing whistle, and almost immediately Buford appeared from the shrubbery and paused, looking to see if it was safe to come out into the clearing. The lumpie held out its bag and shook it vigorously. Lian saw the bag contained several large, very live, very leggy beetles. Buford saw them, too, or smelled them. He hurried over.

At that the lumpie paused and gave the bugs a look of great compassion, then reached deftly into the bag, selected a struggling insect, and held it a few inches from Buford's head. The worm's tongue flicked out and the bug went still. A second flick and the victim was lashed into an orange and toothless mouth. Lian considered throwing up, then remembered she hadn't had breakfast. The lumpie turned and regarded her intently, then gravely offered her a beetle.

· 4 ·

After a conventional breakfast Dr. Farr and Lian walked down to the dig together. Two lumpies ambled on ahead, their moon-round bottoms gleaming in the sunshine. Buford skulked in the underbrush. Twice the walkers had to step aside as a tolat drove past on digging equipment.

"The site is three miles long and not quite two miles wide," Dr. Farr told Lian. "The western end is almost completely buried. We've started digging where structures are closest to the surface. One of the more interesting aspects of the site." He pointed to where the road cut through a hillock. "This earthwork rims the entire eye. We found nothing buried in it, so its purpose probably was not ritual. We don't think it was built for defense; it's much too low. And there is little danger here. It may have been only decorative."

The dirt road made a right turn on the other side of the eye's rim and widened out. Lian noted the trees on the site were much smaller than those outside. Without heavy leaf canopy a profusion of flowering shrubs grew here, and the air smelled of flowers and plowed ground. What she first thought were flakes of colored paper floating about became, on closer look, butterfly-like insects.

The entire area bustled with activity. Tolats were removing the overburden; one machine rolled up sod as if it were strips of carpet; another forked the sod rolls off and deposited them in neat rows to one side of the clearing. Still another unit was shaving the bare ground, layer by layer, and dumping the soil into a carry-all loader for removal. A human stood with map in hand, guiding the operation. Two amalfi worked with power brooms, carefully vacuuming the surface of the now denuded mound.

With the powerful hum of the equipment, the ripping of roots in the soil, the conversations called back and forth in three different languages, half of which were repeated by belt-worn translating units at full volume, the site was almost unbearably noisy to Lian. She was acclimated to long hours alone in the observatory domes where the silence was broken only by the occasional whine of the roof or the telescope turning as a star was tracked.

"Farr? Farr?" The translator crackled as it converted the clicking amalfi tongue. "Lurch your body to my proximity for viewing." Lian looked in the direction of the voice and saw an amalfi gesturing as eagerly as it was possible for it to wave those limp arms.

"Klat appears to have found something," said Dr. Farr. "Let's go look."

They made their way up the slope on a well-defined path and descended into what they thought was once an ancient street. Off to one side, where Klat waited, three tolats were clearing the ground away from an oblong black platform.

"Well done!" said Dr. Farr. "It appears intact."

"What is it?" Lian asked.

"The roof of something, they think," he said. "They're going to dig it out."

"Why not open the roof and look in?"

"There's no seam. It's one piece." Klat and Dr. Farr began debating in esoteric terms whether to dig to the base of this structure first or clear more of the surrounding area to the same level to avoid creating too deep a pit. Everyone else was busy. Lian stood listening, feeling rather out of it. When there was a pause in the conversation, she said, "Would it be all right if I went exploring? Would it be safe?"

"Certainly," said Dr. Farr. "You can't get lost. If you think you are, just follow the sun to the rim of the eye and follow the rim back here."

She picked her way out of the excavation, careful not to step outside the staked walkway, dodging the workers and their equipment, and headed for a path she had seen the lumpies follow off into the woods. Within ten minutes she had left the noise of the excavation behind.

The path meandered along what had once been streets, or so she thought. But it was hard for her to imagine that a city had once stood where she walked now. There was no real trace of it among the trees and bushes and creeping vines. She paused to study the footprints in a sandy spot where rain had washed down from the mounds and found only lumpie tracks and those of wild things. "Strange," she said aloud, thinking someone should have walked this way just out of curiosity.

At the edge of a clearing she paused; the path split, one branch going on through the trees, the other off to the edge of a grassy hill. Then, looking at the hill, she remembered the aerial view of the place and realized this must be the center of the eye.

The slope was deceptively steep. The ground was smooth and slick beneath creeper vine that caught around her ankles and threatened to trip her. By the time she reached the top, she was perspiring and out of breath. She took off her jacket and sat down to rest. The ground was very hard.

She could see the camp from here, and the river winding to the west, the scars of road and excavation hidden by distance and trees. Whoever picked this place for a city chose one of the best places on this world. Mild climate, good scenery . . . it would be nice to build a house up here, she thought. It had been so long since she had even seen a real house. She folded her jacket into a pillow and stretched out on her side, head propped on hand to daydream a bit. Her house would have a beautiful view. Miles and miles of no people, just forest and mountains and the river. Of course, she would have to do something to keep out Buford, the beetles, and their ilk. And at night she could watch the stars.

She wondered what the supernova looked like. She had been looking forward to seeing it. In those final fusion stages was all matter really converted to iron, and could one actually see that happen, then see the iron-red ball blast into pure energy? By the time she got back, it would all be on film, tapes of the past, like any other nova she had ever seen.

Her parents must be so excited, so pleased. It was their prediction that this giant star would nova that had prompted the building of the observatory on this distant world. Lian grinned, remembering how little all the learned papers of envious professional rivals, all the vicious attacks had bothered them. They knew they were right and simply staked their joint and considerable reputations on being so. She wondered if she would ever possess that kind of knowledge and courage.

As she thought about them, she almost envied their passion, their total absorption in the stars. To care so deeply, so exclusively about one's work must be—Lian couldn't even imagine the feeling. But she knew she lacked that degree of caring. She liked astrophysics because they liked it and because she appreciated the poetry of it, the serene order. But with her it was no passion, but a lonely intellectual interest which she sensed would grow tedious with time.

The luxury of self-pity was tempting, but it altered nothing, she decided, and rolled onto her back to enjoy instead the luxury of warm sunshine and grass.

The music crept into her mind without her awareness, almost as part of her daydream. She found herself singing a song she did not know, in words she could not understand. She sat up, frightened, heart beating fast, and heard nothing but the familiar woodland sound.

It's not my imagination, she thought. It's the same song I heard yesterday when we flew over here. But what is it? And am I the only one who hears it? I must be. Wouldn't they have dug here first if they had heard it? If I tell them about it, will they believe me? They really don't know me . . . what if they think I'm crazy?

Lost in thought and more than a little edgy, she made her way off the hill. Why did Dr. Scott think the lumpies might be telepaths? Or did she? Because they lived in the site and she "heard things," too, and suspected the lumpies were responsible?

Lian almost bumped into the lumpie before she saw it. It was standing erect and quite still in the shrubs at the rim of the hill, watching her as if it expected her to talk to it. On impulse, she hummed the song she had just heard.

A dim, glazed expression entered the lumpie's eyes, as if she had confused it. It tilted its head, and the smiling mouth opened slightly. It had small white teeth, almost human in shape. She repeated the song. The lumpie listened.

When she had finished, it waved its anemone-like fingers very rapidly and nodded its head. And then it did something that both frightened and excited her. From deep in its throat it began to sing in rich round tones that seemed to trace a pattern in the mind. It repeated the simple melody Lian had hummed, corrected and enriched it and sent it soaring through the trees. Then it stopped abruptly and looked around, as if afraid someone else had heard, its distress so evident that Lian felt nervous sympathy for it.

"It's all right," she said. "There's no one else here."

The lumpie looked at her, and she felt helpless to soothe it. And all the time her mind was wondering, Was this a song or language? Intelligence or an instinctive territorial call? But if that, then why this evident fear of self-betrayal? Fear of whom or what? The archaeologists?

Some carnivore attracted by the sound? And how had she first heard this song from the air?

There was a rustle of twigs and scrunching leaves. Both she and her companion turned to see two other lumpies running toward them. There was much urgent finger waving, and the three surrounded her. A cool, soft anemone hand reached out and touched her arm. She flinched away, startled, and then felt ashamed of her rudeness. They all regarded her now, then slowly backed away. Somehow she got the feeling she had just become a great disappointment, as if they had expected more from her.

The three looked at one another, then turned away and started off down the path, walking slowly. They did not look back. After hesitating a moment to argue with her common sense, she followed.

· *5* ·

The lumpies led her to the far side of the hill, down through a thicket, and beside an oblong meadow bare of trees. They seemed in no hurry, almost aimless.

Orange berries grew at the meadow's edge. They stopped to pick and eat them. Their fingers were very deft. When they moved on, it was to wander downhill into a heavily wooded area.

Vines flourished over a low cliff. The three left the path and approached the cliff, pushed aside some vines, and disappeared behind them. Lian stopped and waited, watching to see where they would re-emerge. But they did not, and when some minutes passed, she decided they had grown tired of being followed and had given her the slip. And very neatly, too.

She imagined this trio of chubby gray creatures tiptoeing away into the woods and smiled at the image. She walked up the slope to investigate, but slowly, just in case they were hiding back there, watching her. She did not want to irritate or startle them. Even gentle animals bit when provoked.

"Hello?" she called and patted the vines.

There was no response. Birds sang among the trees.

She pulled some vines aside and saw a cavelike hollow space behind them. The lumpies were not there. She slipped inside and let the vines fall shut. Gravel scrunched beneath her boots. It was a pleasant hiding place. The sunlit leaves made an opaque wall of jade that shadowed green on green. The cliff narrowed down to nothing to her right. She turned left and followed the tunnel-like curve of the outcropping. Around the second bend she saw an opening in the cliff wall and stopped still.

It was a doorway, perfectly round and machine tooled, as if designed for a huge vault. A few yards away, almost buried in soil and leaves, lay the massive door that had once fit that frame. Lian stood there, taking in the meaning of it all, then reached over and knocked on the cliff wall. It rang not as stone but as a foamed metal, part of the ruin. Lumpies went through that doorway; she could see their finger marks all over it.

Her first impulse was to run back to the dig and tell Dr. Farr. But tell him what—"I found an open door"? That sounded rather silly even to consider. Besides, they probably knew about it. He said they had sonar-tested and measured the whole site. Probably it was only a wall remaining from a ruin and not exciting at all. Still, there were no human tracks. She went up to have a look, thinking, That's how the lumpies gave me the slip.

The door led into a ruin, but not the ruin she expected. It opened on a wide, dim corridor that stretched away into darkness. Its floor was covered with mud and leaves. Lumpie tracks were everywhere, and the vaulted walls were hand-marked as high as they could reach. One glance and Lian knew she had made an important find.

"I wonder where it goes," she whispered to herself. "To the center of the eye?" It would be interesting to learn what was under that green hill, learn it by herself without having to explain about the singing to people who might not believe her.

The lumpies must have come in here; it couldn't be too dangerous or they wouldn't go in and out. And it must be here that they had learned to sing. She checked to see that nothing lurked on either side of the doorway and then entered. It was very still inside. There was a cellar smell of dampness and age.

"Hello?" she called. There was no echo. These walls were as sound-absorptive as the corridors of a starship. "Lumpies? Are you in there?"

If they were, they weren't answering.

Lian set off down the hall, walking almost on tiptoe. Between every other support beam was a closed door, like an oddly shaped hatch. She did not want to touch them for fear one would fall on her, as the outer door had fallen off. After about three minutes she turned and looked back. It seemed a long way to the entrance. Suppose there was something alive in here. Suppose the roof was ready to collapse. Her footsteps slowed.

Suddenly they loomed up out of the shadows, their eyes shining gray with reflected light from the distant door. She gave a yelp of fright and ran. They did not chase her. Afterward she was not sure why she stopped running, except that she knew they meant no harm and had only been waiting for her. She turned back to join them.

They led her through dark hallways and down dim corridors, past shadowy things vaguely seen, and none of it recognizable. Only a faint glow from the ceiling overhead kept her from feeling trapped in a labyrinth. As they went deeper into the ruins, passageways stood open, dark and mysterious. Twice she saw what could have been wall murals, but it was too dark to be sure.

The passageway ended. In the dim light she could see no door or branching hall. Her guides stopped as if confused, and exchanged finger signs, then sat on their haunches and looked at one another.

"What is it?" said Lian. "Is this what you wanted to show me?" They smiled their clown smiles, then turned to look at the wall again. She felt a flicker of irritation and disappointment and at the same time understood Dr. Scott's remark about their playing the fool.

But that was unfair of her, she decided. They had already given her the knowledge of the existence of this place. What more did she expect? Or want? Ruins were of no real interest to her.

But she did expect more, even if she wasn't sure what. She stepped around the lumpies and approached the wall. Directly past them the floor began to slant, ramplike. One did not usually find walls built across ramps, but one often found security gates at the top of ramps. If that was what this was, then her exploration in here was ended. With no power source to move it, the gate would never open.

But its existence would be of interest to the archaeologists. She ran her hands along the rough texture of the wall and found a seam and then a frame that reached from the floor to as high as she could stretch. She checked the wall on the other side of the ramp, and as she felt for the matching seam, her fingers struck against a switch plate.

It was too dark to see what it looked like. There were holes in it, a radial design, perhaps a plug of some sort. She looked back at the lumpies, wondering if they knew it was a security gate—or if they knew what lay behind it. One lumpie got up slowly and came over to join her. At close range it smelled of grass and berries and a mustard-like scent of its own. It stood erect, peered nearsightedly at the thing her touch had found, then reached past her and fit its fingertips into the holes.

"Very good!" she said, and then was interrupted by the hum of a motor. A faint crack of light appeared along the floor and grew slowly higher. "This can't be!" Lian informed the trio, who gazed at the light in wide-eyed simpleness, the one beside her with its hand still on the switch. "What's in there?" She reached up and pulled that supple hand away from the switch plate. The gate continued to rise. She began to back away, just in case. It was probably an old power cell still functioning by freakish circumstances . . . but just in case there was anything alive . . .

There was not.

The Counter looked out upon a small and rather monstrous alien and three of its responsibilities. It hummed the greeting signal.

6

Lian saw a great amphitheater, the center of it occupied by what looked like a massive and very elaborate computer. Glassed booths lined the circular walls. Opaque green glass covered the dome. Looking up at the light patches caused by disarrayed soil and vines, she recognized the trail of her footsteps up and down that dome and the spot where she had rested. A shiver went over her. From here that roof looked very thin.

The air rushing past them to escape down the dark hallway felt warm and dry. It smelled of machinery and dust and some aged sweetness. Hidden speakers whispered a song of eight notes, paused, then repeated at slightly louder volume, paused, then repeated again, like an alarm signal, or a coda.

Dust in the recording device crackled in amplifiers. Dust covered the endless expanse of blue floor. Dusty cameras like huge eyes peered at them from either side of the gateway. They were being greeted and recorded by some still-functioning relic from the past.

The lumpie beside her inhaled deeply, as if it had been holding its breath, and moved closer to her. It looked so worried she impulsively put her arm around its shoulders and found it was a solid creature and as nice to touch as a very expensive leather glove. She hugged, then patted it reassuringly. "It's all right," she said. "It's all machinery. Nothing will harm us if we're careful."

Something brushed against her right hand, then twined through her fingers. She glanced down to find herself holding hands with the other lumpie, who was also holding hands with the third.

"I'm sure we all feel safer now," she said, and laughed at the thought of the picture they must make. "It would be nicer, of course, if we could talk it over. But since we can't, I will talk and you can all smile. It will be just like home."

The lumpies looked at her.

"The first thing we must do if we're going inside is make sure we can get back out. That means we must secure this door." She freed herself from their huddling and looked about for something with which to wedge the track. Some distance down the hall lay a pile of rubble. From it she selected a sturdy strip of metal and tugged it back across the floor to the ramp. It was too heavy to lift. The lumpies watched her, wide-eyed.

"Thank you all," she said as she shoved the wedge into place at an angle against the gate track. "I couldn't have done it without you." She hand-measured to make sure there was enough room for her to squeeze through that space if the gate slid down upon the wedge. Then she gauged the girth of the largest of her companions and hoped for the best.

"Come," she invited them. "Let's go see who lived here."

She walked down the ramp, out onto the floor of the dome, and stood there for a moment, hands on hips, surveying the area. It looked alien, but not as alien as it would have to most people. Lian had spent a good part of her life in enclosures very much like this where humans were dwarfed by space, tile, and glass barrenness and elaborate machinery. All that was lacking here was the giant telescope, angled skyward.

The click of her boot heels on the floor was firm and sure of itself.

Camera eyes followed her as she made a slow circle of the place, peering into the glass booths at the dials and terminal boards.

"It seems to be a central control room," she called to her three followers, who had advanced as far as the ramp's end and stood watching. "Some of the dials and gauges are still registering. Perhaps this was the power plant for the city . . . but why so intricate for a city so small?"

Every so often along the curved wall there was a switch panel like the one at the ramp gate. On impulse she placed her hands palm to palm and tried to approximate a lumpie finger arrangement, then touched the plate. Her fingers were too broadly tipped and would not fit. But a lumpie hand would. She gave them a speculative glance, then went over and held out her hand to the one who had opened the door. "I need you," she said. "Don't give me a soulful look. I just want to know something. It won't hurt you."

Very reluctantly the lumpie took her hand and accompanied her to the nearest booth, where she fit its hand to the switch plate. Two yards to the right a glass panel slid open. Even though she had suspected it, she found it hard to believe.

"It's yours?" she whispered. "You lived here . . ." She stared, perplexed, at this wide-eyed creature, who returned the stare. "What have you done with it? What have you done to yourselves? You're not simple-minded! You're not animals . . . you are . . ." She released its hand, and the creature galloped across the floor to rejoin its companions at the end of the ramp. From that point they continued to watch her.

But what were they? Masters—or servants of a superior race? None had been in here in—how long? Or maybe the configuration of this switch that fit a lumpie touch was only circumstance and she had not only jumped but made a quantum leap to conclusions.

In the background the speakers still repeated those eight notes, and absentmindedly she whistled them. The speaker shut off in mid-note.

"I will talk and you can all smile. It will be just like home!" She whirled around. It was a computer's voice, not a replay of a recording of her own speech, but the unit's eerie mimicry without understanding. "I will talk and you can all smile," it repeated. She walked over for a closer look.

"Go ahead and talk," she said, but the computer did not.

The central unit was sheathed in anodized gold and for most of its length was covered by a domed transparent housing. Its design was more elegant than the newest of tolat computers, yet Lian suspected this unit had been functioning since long before the first tolat computer existed. There was a distinct wheeze as its air-intake ducts came on, but what appeared to be a spectrograph was analyzing the chemical components of something. The ratios looked familiar, and she wondered if it was analyzing her breath.

She wondered, too, if it contained a translator. If the race which had built it came from another planet, as Dr. Farr had said they might . . . Turning to face a camera eye, she held up the appropriate number of fingers and began to count. "One, two, three, four—" and then stopped. This was a silly waste of time. If the computer could translate, she would need a year to program it verbally. The tolats would figure it out and translate the language on their own units.

She decided she had better head back to the dig to report before Dr. Farr decided she was lost again. Besides, this was all a little too much to take in and comprehend at one time. She yawned, a wide yawn, half from fatigue and half from nerves. The snake's head of a camera focused on her mouth and lurched sideways as she politely covered the yawn with her hand.

"I'm an omnivorous mammal, sentient, and in an adolescent stage," she said, "if you really care." Then, noticing her sleeve was dirty, she began to brush it off as she circled the computer for a total view of it before leaving. At the far end was an oddly shaped opening, wide and black as a cave mouth into the computer's interior. Without slowing her pace, she detoured closer to look inside.

It sucked her in as a black hole pulls in the mass of a star orbiting too near. Only half of her scream escaped.

· 7 ·

The Counter could not remember such an intractable specimen. Even though its appendages were held immobile, it persisted in ordering them to act, wasting valuable time. It was difficult to do a proper analysis.

The specimen's first reaction was fear, an emotion familiar to the Counter from past experience with the people. Its next emotion was anger. That was new and very interesting. This thing totally resented being analyzed, considered it in some abstract way a violation of its entire unit, and at the same time, helpless though it was, it counted on release and planned retribution to the violator.

The Counter paused to consider this factor. It found it illogical but perhaps useful for the unit's ultimate survival.

The unit was partially encased in synthetic fibers, acidic long-chain monomers. Its natural covering was far·more complex. The Counter took cell samples and noted the puncture of this covering to obtain a liquid sample of the interior was met with new anger by the specimen.

The Counter's low power source was rapidly being drained by the specimen's struggles. The Counter administered a relaxant charge; the mind responded with more or less rational thought images. Could the Counter have smiled, it would have, for it found this mind's current overwhelming urge was to find a way to communicate with the Counter.

The Counter did a thorough search of the memory banks of the alien mind, recorded this data for later analysis, paid particular interest to its data on astrophysics, noted the unit's prolonged sense of isolation from its own kind, and its seemingly resultant affection for other living creatures.

Before releasing the specimen, the Counter assimilated its language codes. It was possible the specimen could be taught a basic understanding of the people's language . . . if the Counter could get the people to speak again. The specimen could not be reprogrammed to adequately absorb and convert radiant impulses; its existing equipment transmitted but only partially received. The Counter regretted this; it would have greatly simplified communication.

Once it could have transposed, translated, and speaker-communicated with this alien in a matter of hours. Now, in this aged and diminished state, with not even a fraction of its normal power, that seemed beyond the cells' capacity. Still, if given time to think it over, perhaps, like its people, the Counter could talk again.

· 8 ·

One moment she was wrapped in blackness, dreaming; the next she was out and standing some distance from the computer. The three lumpies were beside her, patting her hands and peering over her, as if to make sure she was unharmed. She let them pat as she tried to remember what had happened, why she had dreamed all those things forgotten years ago. That computer thought . . . talked . . . ? Was it a medical unit fifty generations advanced? Or more . . .

The largest lumpie made a moaning noise and touched her left arm. She glanced down and saw a very neat hole in her white sleeve. Beneath the hole blood was beginning to clot on a deep and sore abrasion.

"It took a sample of me!" She was indignant, then something else occurred to her. "What are you three doing in here? You were too scared to come beyond the ramp before. Did you come to help me?"

They did not answer, but the smallest one took her wounded arm, splayed its fingers around the biceps and applied gentle pressure. As it did so, she watched its face. The eyes narrowed as it concentrated on the wound; the face lost its clownlike expression and became still with some kind of knowing. The soreness went away, and as she watched, the discoloration around the wound cleared.

"Hypnosis?" she said as the lumpie released her. "Or are you an empathist? If you can do that . . ." She pointed to her black eye. "That hurts, too."

The trio studied her face, and there was a rapid exchange of finger signaling. The small lumpie pointed to her eye, then to her cheek and lip, and then to the left eye. There was more finger waving.

Lian felt her knees beginning to shake in a delayed reaction from the fear of being trapped by the computer. "If you'll excuse me," she said, staggered a few steps past them, and sat down on the floor.

The consultation ended. All three dropped to their feet and padded over; the self-appointed healer explored the left side of her face with its fingers. It was like being touched by tiny soft erasers. She closed her eyes and took a deep breath. The erasers hesitated, then continued. After a few seconds she tried to open her eyes, and fingers gently pushed the lids down again.

She sat there, not really thinking, yet with a dozen different impressions going through her mind. Why did she trust the lumpies like this when she would not have allowed a similarly strange human to touch her? They needed names; she could not continue thinking of them as big and small and medium. And why did *that thing* want her language if it wasn't going to talk? Perhaps she was going mad and none of this had happened.

"That's enough, thank you," she said, and opened her eyes. "I want to get out of here now. I have had quite enough for today. I am an astrophysicist, not a guardian. . . ." She paused, wondering why she had used the word "guardian" when *they* were attempting to take care of *her.*

She stood up rather unsteadily and began to walk out. The lumpies followed, still looking anxious. The cameras watched them cross the floor and exit up the ramp. At the gate she paused, then stopped to tug the wedge away from the track. Without a word, a lumpie touched the switch and the gate slid shut behind them.

"Perhaps you already have names," she said as they retraced their route through the ruined hallways. "But I don't know them. So please don't be insulted . . . if you understand. . . . You are Cuddles, because you do that a lot," she told the largest of the three. "You, my small healer, are Poonie. And our switch operator is Naldo."

They padded along beside her, their stubby gray feet almost noiseless compared to her two booted heels, their eyes sure in the dimness that made her stumble. When she repeated their names, touching the shoulder of each one as she did so, they smiled up at her, sweet, vacuous smiles, all the knowing that had briefly appeared before now lacking. Lian felt a great urge to cry without knowing quite why. She decided it was nervous exhaustion from being so frightened.

It felt very good to emerge into the sunlight again. From the bottom of the hill, looking back at the vine-covered cliff, she found it hard to believe what lay behind it. The sun's position told her it was long past noon. She headed back toward the dig, thinking of all she had to report.

"Dr. Farr is going to be so excited!" she said, remembering the undisturbed dust on that floor. Suddenly she noticed there were no footsteps behind her. She turned. The lumpies were nowhere in sight.

"Poonie?" she called. "Naldo?"

"Lian? It's Scotty. Lian? Is that you?" Dr. Scott came hurrying along the path, looking worried. "Who were you calling?"

"Lumpies. They were right behind me. . . ."

"Where did they go?" Then without waiting for an answer, "And where did they get those names?"

Lian shrugged, half embarrassed. "Me."

"Why not?" Dr. Scott was staring at Lian's face. "Forgive me, but you heal very quickly! The swelling's gone from your eye since this morning. There's only a little bruise left on the corner."

"I thought it felt better," Lian said, not wanting to explain it all at the moment, not wanting to betray. "Did you think I was lost? Is that why you were looking for me?"

"Oh, no. It's lunchtime, and we thought maybe your watch was broken in the crash. Did you see anything interesting this morning?"

"I've been . . . all over." Lian hardly knew where to begin, and she no longer was sure she wanted to. It wasn't that she didn't like Dr. Farr or Dr. Scott, but none of this was really her responsibility—not the dig or the lumpies. . . . She would be here less than a week, and then she would never see any of them again. She would go back to the observatory, back to working and studying alone, back to where, if she was late, nobody noticed she was missing. Not even a lumpie.

"Dr. Scott—uh—Scotty, how much do you know about lumpies?"

"Why?"

"I want to know. Actual facts. Not feelings."

"They can weave—I told you that. They seem friendly. None of them bite." She paused to think. "They eat fruits and berries and roots. They are very clean. They go swimming in the river in the morning and again before dark. If they weren't so large, they would make perfect pets. As you probably have decided, judging by the names you've given them."

"Do they hunt?"

"I don't think so. I don't think they like meat. Or perhaps they're afraid to kill things. When the bidernecks—they're ugly little batlike—"

"I've seen them."

"Well, sometimes they go after a lumpie."

"They eat them?" Lian was horrified.

"No. The odd thing is, they don't. They just seem to like to torment the lumpies. A whole flock will land on one animal, crawl all over it, making a screeching fuss. But they won't bite it more than once, and then only slightly. The other lumpies will drive them off and then stand there with tears running down their faces. It's a very pathetic sight. I saw it happen twice, and I'm not sure, because it's hard for me to tell the animals apart, but I don't believe I've seen either victim of the harassment afterward."

Lian thought that over. "Maybe those two lumpies were dying?"

"Why would you think a thing like that? They died of trauma from being attacked, you mean?" She frowned. "Do you think lumpies are that sensitive?"

"No. Well—maybe? Bidernecks frighten me."

She didn't want to say what she really thought and what suspicions of hers this story might confirm. As scavengers the bidernecks could smell illness in a creature—the scent of a fever, the sweetness of hemorrhage. They were genetically coded to recognize weakness, anticipate death. But they could not digest species alien to their world. If the lumpies knew this . . . it was possible they had come to recognize an attack by bidernecks as a sign of approaching death and wept to see it.

It was also possible that the lumpies were timid and cried because the bidernecks frightened them. Still, the lumpies had come to help her. . . .

"Have you ever heard anything sing around here?"

"Have you?"

"Yes, today," Lian said. "Have you?"

Dr. Scott didn't answer right away, and when she did, her words seemed very deliberate. "There is a place in these woods, beyond the spot where we met back there . . . I was walking alone one evening . . . the first day we were here. I was watching the sky, glad to be out of it . . . glad to be alone for a change. . . ." She stopped and they walked in silence for a bit.

"And?" Lian prompted her after a polite interval.

"I don't know what. A low, mournful song, very long, with infinite variations on a single involved theme. It made sense—mathematically, anyway . . . the moons were up, the shadows were dark. When the wind made the trees move, the shadows changed."

"Were you scared?"

"I was terrified," Dr. Scott said. "And I don't know why, Lian, but it seemed to me then—and it still does now that I think about it—that the song was sung by something at least as intelligent as ourselves. Perhaps that is what frightened me—that idea." She shook her head and smiled apologetically. "I don't like to remember that. Did it affect you the same way?"

"Is that why you came out to find me? Because you were frightened here?"

"No . . . well, maybe a little. But did you hear a song like that?"

"No," Lian said. "But I heard a song. Like a greeting, or maybe just an everyday song. Has anyone else heard singing out here?"

"If they have, no one has mentioned it, and I didn't want to bring it up for fear of scaring people unnecessarily. It's an unknown . . . what do you think it was?"

Lian shrugged. "A lumpie?" Her voice was almost wistful with hope. Dr. Scott started to laugh and then saw Lian was serious.

"Why?" she said, too gently, a small worry entering her eyes.

"Because." Lian wasn't going to risk being laughed at again. "I . . just do. Is Dr. Farr still at the dig?"

· 9 ·

·

They arrived back at the dig in time to hear a chorus of "ahs!" Dr. Farr and the others stood on the bank watching two tolats in the pit below. They were trying to cut a hole in the wall of one of the two square structures they had unearthed.

They were using torches designed to cut through the most exotic and resistant of metals or metallic plastics. But whatever this particular substance was, it not only was not cutting, it was deflecting beams so powerful their heat made the exposed red clay boil like magma.

It was hard to tell who was most excited: Dr. Farr, who saw in this indication of an ancient race with a highly advanced technology and possibly a civilization to match; Klat, who immediately wanted the substance analyzed to learn if it was derived from amalfi technology; or the tolats, who looked upon this resistant substance as an engineering problem to be analyzed, solved, and forgotten.

Lian had come back with the full intention of telling Dr. Farr all about her discovery. But now as she stood there listening to all the divergent opinions, she realized that to tell Dr. Farr would be to tell the entire staff. Diplomat that he was, he would include everyone to avoid bitter professional jealousies and general ill feelings among staff members. And that would be not only right but necessary for the harmony of the expedition.

She trusted him but not all the expedition crew. She knew nothing about them. If she talked too much . . . suppose the tolats decided to analyze a lumpie by testing its mental and physical capabilities or even dissecting one or more. This was legally a Class Five world; the lumpies were officially "wildlife," vulnerable animals. They could be hunted, by permit, or collected for zoos.

There was no way she could report what she found without involving the lumpies. If she omitted all mention of them, one look at the interior of the place, with lumpie tracks and finger marks all over, would show they had entered there. The staff might think nothing of that if it were not for the switch plates and, above all, how she had gained access to the dome. These were all educated people; if it was obvious to a complete amateur that the buildings showed a link between lumpie and ruin, it would be more obvious to an expert.

They are going to find out sooner or later, her common sense reminded her, but not because I betrayed the lumpies or their old computer.

"Lian! There you are," Dr. Farr called, and she jumped as if he could read her mind. He came up the walkway to join her. "Did you find the site interesting?"

"Very. I walked quite a distance."

"Find any artifacts on the surface?"

"No," she said honestly.

He nodded. "That's the curious thing about this place. There are no artifacts. No middens. Just structures. It's almost as if it were a model city. As if no one ever lived here. Fascinating, but"—he stared off into the pit—"a bit discouraging at times."

Lian thought how easy it would be to cheer him up and how much of a relief. "Dr. Farr?" she began, then stopped. If the lumpies had wanted to tell somebody else, they would have.

Something in her expression made him regard her more closely. If she told . . . it would be to please him and to ease her own sense of responsibility toward the lumpies—hardly admirable motives. "I—uh —would you please tell Scotty I've gone up to camp to have my lunch?"

One of the man's eyebrows raised questioningly, but all he said was, "Certainly." She had the feeling he was watching her halfway up the road.

Before eating, she went to her quarters to shower and change. Her clothing had become dusty and grass stained during her morning jaunt, and she was unaccustomed to grime of any sort. Observatories were almost surgically clean places. En route to the dining hall, she put the soiled garments into the autocleaner and paused for a moment to watch them writhe.

The dining hall was empty. She took a sandwich and a cube of fruit drink from the dispenser and wandered outside to sit on the grass and eat. That was a mistake. Within seconds a wortle marched around a dome and headed in her direction. Others followed. They formed in review before her, owlish eyes watching each bite she took, wide beaks working over each bite denied them. She went on eating.

Thinking perhaps she wasn't getting the hint, one bird hopped up on her knee and stared from closer range. It was heavy and its claws dug in. She moved to dislodge him, and in that instant another wortle stole her sandwich. The thief in blue feather pants hurried off with its booty, the other wortles giving chase.

"It's not a very good sandwich," Lian called after them. "But compared to the taste of beetles, you may like it."

She sat there to finish the fruit drink, and before long the wortles were straggling back. Liquids apparently held no charms for them.

They stared at her awhile, then began to yawn great frog-mouth yawns. One by one they closed their eyes and dozed in the sun. Seeing them was very suggestive. On this revised time schedule an afternoon nap seemed an excellent idea and the lush grass an inviting bed. But remembering the beetles and Buford, she went to her room to sleep.

When Dr. Farr woke her, the sun was low and her room glowed with diffused pink light. "Would you care to walk down to the river and watch the lumpies swim?" he said. "I admit it's not exciting, but we take our entertainment where we can on an expedition."

She glanced at her watch. "Do we have time before dinner?" She was very hungry.

"Dinner is fashionably late here. It fills up a long evening."

They followed a switchback path down through the bushes on the hillside past a series of burrows where the wortle colony lived. Below, some of the staff was already sitting on the rocks. The sound of a miniature landslide from the sandy bluff caused Lian to look back to see a lone tolat coming down the hill. The tolat's eyes were erect to see over the bushes.

"Shall we wait for it?" she asked Dr. Farr. "To be polite? It's all by itself, and it might like company."

"Very well," he said agreeably. "But I doubt if the gesture will be appreciated. Tolats are very different from you and me."

She interpreted the remark as fact. The tolat caught up to them as they stood waiting for it. It swerved past without speaking, without so much as a glance at them, and went on down the path as if they were not there. Seeing her puzzled expression, Dr. Farr said, "It was a kind thought, Lian. By human standards. But by tolat standards, our colleague was not rude."

"It could at least say good evening."

Dr. Farr smiled. "To a tolat that is an unessential remark and a foolish waste of time. I said good evening to one on a night when it was raining—it promptly went to its superior to question my mental fitness."

The lumpies, some sixty of them, swam from a gravel sandbar a short distance away from the rocks. For the first time Lian saw they came in all ages. She was going to remark aloud on that and stopped herself; of course they had young. But it pleased her to see it nonetheless. The two of them sat down to watch.

"How do you tell male from female?"

"We can't," said Dr. Scott, who sat nearby. "They all look alike. Only another lumpie knows."

Almost the entire expedition crew was watching the creatures, envying them the pleasure of the river. Swimming in untreated water was off limits to the staff. There was always the danger of foreign parasites that might cause exotic illnesses as yet undiagnosed and untreatable by preprogrammed medical computers.

To see a lumpie swim was to see the creature in a different concept. The water turned them into creatures of grace. They looked like seals in the river, plump and sleek and fast. Heads out and up, rear legs tight together, arms paddling, forelegs balancing and guiding like flippers, they played tag and rolled and arabesqued over and over. And it was an entertaining performance.

"Who named them lumpies?" Lian asked after watching their water acrobatics. "It's a very derogatory name. I think they're beautiful."

Several staff members laughed.

Dr. Scott spoke up. "I think they are, too, once you get used to them. Lumpie is an ancient provincialism from the mining areas of the North American Midwest. I believe it referred to the poor who scavenged lumps of coal in and around the mines, coal the machinery could not recover or wasted. Inadequate diet often made these people obese and rather dull-witted. The term has come down through the centuries to mean a stupid but harmless animal or person. My guess would be that these creatures were named lumpies by one of the first ore freighter crewmen to visit this planet, and the name stuck, as cruel but superficially apt nicknames do."

Lian regarded her with new interest. "Do you think the lumpies are smart?"

"When I watch the joy they take in swimming, yes," she said. "They certainly are charming animals."

"We of the planet Tola do not trust any . . . (untranslatable)," said a tolat standing behind them. The speaker on its translator amplified the hiss of its voice. "Not when we are ignorant of their habits and hungers. You unshelled ones are far too soft. . . ."

Considering the benign appearance of lumpies versus the formidable looks of a tolat, Lian thought that an odd statement. How could a lumpie hurt a tolat, short of sitting on it? Then, in an effort to be fair, she thought she probably was prejudiced because, like the lumpies, she too could walk upright and smiled and cried and was unshelled. One always had to allow for the chauvinism peculiar to individual races and species.

To her, tolats were so uncomfortably crablike, with their quick scuttling movements, their eyes like oblong blue gems on sticks that lifted up and out or retracted into neat slots in their shelled bodies. To watch them walk, bowl-like body suspended between four matched pairs of jointed legs, was to see synchronization as an art form. To watch them eat, delicately shredding their food with foreclaws and with exquisite precision inserting the bits into their wedge-shaped mouths, did strange things to Lian's stomach. It was, of course, impolite to say this, since tolats probably found the feeding apparatus of humans equally revolting.

When the sun almost touched the horizon, the lumpies began to leave the beach in groups of three or four. The last of the swimmers came ashore and stood looking at the water, as if making sure everyone was safely out. One small lumpie turned to observe the observers, then reached over to touch a friend and pointed toward their audience. Too quickly, as if to cover the gesture, Lian thought, the friend or parent caught the other's hand and they hurried off together into the woods with the rest of the group.

"Wasn't that cute?" someone said, and there was nervous laughter from the staff; they had not enjoyed being observed.

Why was that funny? Lian wondered, her glance flicking over her companions. Of all the species she might encounter in the twilight, any but the humans would terrify her. And she wasn't sure about the humans.

No matter who or what they were, Lian thought, most sentient creatures felt the need to feel superior to the others. She never understood why. Her father said it was a question of dominance; her mother said Lian was being unfair and would understand when she was older and had the responsibility of a staff of her own. But this was one of those things Lian did not want to understand because she suspected that when she did, it would make her very sad. Without waiting for the others, she slid off the rock and started up the path.

Dew was rising. Among the shrubs night-blooming flowers were opening and scenting the air. The wortles were muttering in their dark burrows. Insects sang. From across the river something called three flute notes and liked them so well it repeated them over and over.

"There's a big star!" a human voice called, and the hills echoed, "Star—star—star." The line of people ascending the path stopped, and faces turned to the north to look at this beauty, coolly glittering high above the horizon.

"Make a wish."

"It's a good omen."

"It must mean a successful expedition." Dr. Farr's remark was greeted with appreciative murmurings.

Lian looked and with an odd little twinge of pain recognized the beautiful star for what it was—the supernova, the fiery death of a distant sun. She was going to tell them that, then decided not to. People did not always appreciate raw facts—especially when they were engaged in making wishes.

"You must have wished something important," said Scotty. "You look so serious."

"I was wishing I had a telescope," she said, and gave her a lumpie smile.

· 𝟭𝟬 ·

"I'm afraid you're going to find your visit with us rather dull," Dr. Farr said at dinner that evening. "Especially so compared to what you're missing by being away from the observatory. That must be very disappointing to you."

"It's disappointing," Lian said, thinking disappointment was not the right word, and feeling guilty. The truth was that, from the time she heard the lumpie sing, she hadn't thought of the supernova until she saw it from the river path. "But being here is very nice. Being *alive* is very nice. Until I started to crash I never thought about . . . not being." It gave her an odd feeling to think of her own death, and she quickly changed the subject. "Did you ever find a way into the buildings you dug up?"

"Not yet. The engineers took sonar photos this afternoon. Penetration was poor. The structures seem to house equipment of some sort."

"That must have excited the tolats," said Lian.

Scotty laughed. "You've noticed they like that sort of thing, have you? They loved it, but it rather discouraged the rest of us."

"I think we'll spend another day at our present dig, and if it continues to be unproductive, we'll move to the center of the eye," said Dr. Farr. "I can't help feeling the design of this place may have served some ritual purpose and that, if we are to discover what it was, we should work in that area."

"Really?" said Lian carefully, as she forked up mashed turkey. "Why didn't you start digging there first?"

"Several reasons. Our initial aerial tests indicated the big mound was solid. Now that we've seen the actual construction of one of their buildings, we know our testing equipment may be completely inadequate, that the hill may well be hollow. Another reason is that religious ritual holds very little interest for our nonhuman colleagues. Because their cultures include no form of superstition or faith, they accord it no importance."

"You think the hill is a temple?" said Lian.

"Perhaps, in some aspects, if the shape of the eye holds any ritual significance. Or it might be a sports arena. In any case, I hope it's roofed with less durable material than that we've already found."

"Tomorrow," said Scotty, "if we dig down to street level and find nothing, what are we going to do?"

"At the present site, nothing. We don't have the time or budget to waste."

"Then in the afternoon I think I'll take Lian to see the lumpie colony."

"Of course. Do you find them of particular interest?" he asked Lian.

"I think they are . . . very endearing."

He thought that over. "Yes. I suppose so. Animals have never had much appeal for me. They are so physical. One spends a great deal of time averting one's gaze from the more intimate details of their lives. Though I must admit your lumpies are more circumspect than the average animal."

"Including most humans," said Scotty, and won Lian's full approval.

The supernova was the brightest star framed by her round window that night. She lay with hands clasped behind her head and stared up at the stars with unseeing eyes. The strangest night sounds went unheeded. Her feet were cold; she raised them, stiff-legged, and tucked the blanket under them.

Should she continue to gamble on the slim chance that they would never find the door into the ruin? They had been here six weeks without finding it. If the ruin did belong to the lumpies and the lumpies wanted to be "discovered," surely they would have managed to attract the archaeologists' attention.

But then she reasoned, if a gentle gorilla took a human by the arm and signed, "Come see my house," the human would run screaming —as much afraid of the unsuspected and unwanted intelligence as of the gesture of familiarity. It was probable that lumpies had attempted to establish contact with humans and had been rebuffed.

She was thinking of the cargo men at Limai talking about the lumpies when she suddenly remembered a sofa in the Port Director's office, a sofa upholstered in fine gray leather. "One of my men made it for me," the Director had said. "Beautiful, isn't it? All local stuff."

If that leather was what she now suspected it to be, no laws had been broken. Balthor was a Class Five world; hunting was allowed. To prove lumpies were an intelligent species would grant them automatic protection under Federation law. But Balthor was a frontier world, Limai a frontier outpost—a place that appealed to people who could not conform to normal societies: misfits, drifters, men searching for alien wealth in any form. Who could enforce those laws out here if anyone decided to violate them? Yet, if the lumpies were discovered now, and they probably would be, those laws and common decency would be their only chance.

By her silence she had assumed responsibility. Time was short. She had to find some definite proof of lumpie intelligence—anything that would place them in the sentient being category. Art, tools, furniture —something had to be there, something that gave the creatures legal protection and ownership to what she felt was theirs. If she found that, then in good conscience she could tell Dr. Farr and the others of her discovery.

Thoughts sank deeper into dream, and in sleep she pulled her numb arms beneath the blanket and curled up into comfort.

Her wrist alarm went off at six, and she was awake. The smallest of Balthor's four moons was a lemon sliver in the north, the sun was almost up, and the wortles were out. The beach by the river was deserted; either it was too chilly or lumpies were not early risers.

There were only a few tolats in the dining room. None acknowledged her greeting, but then neither did they speak to one another. She was going to take her food outside to eat, then remembered the wortles and sat at the table facing the window. On her way out she stopped at the message board by the door and wrote: "Dr. Farr, have gone exploring. Will be back for lunch. Lian."

At the dig the tolats were already at work. The chatter of their jackhammers echoed through the woods. Lian stopped to watch; the bit couldn't chip a fragment out of the wall. In a lull in the noise she heard them explode into hissed sibilants and wondered if they were swearing in frustration.

The racket resumed and followed her down the path, muffled only slightly by trees or distance. If anything was being broadcast by the computer, she failed to hear it as she passed the dome. The whole site seemed deserted by wildlife, driven off by the angry throb of the drill.

Perhaps because of the noise, she saw them first. They were waiting for her by the end of the long meadow—Naldo, Poonie, and Cuddles, sitting on the grass, smiling and nodding at one another. Each time the distant jackhammers chattered, they jumped.

Lian was surprised, not so much by the fact that they were there as by the degree of her own pleasure in seeing them. She was wondering why that was, when they turned, saw her, and came to meet her in a glad hustle.

"Where did you go yesterday?" she asked without expecting an answer, touching fingertips with them in greeting. "Scotty wouldn't hurt you."

Poonie stood up and peered at her face, examining the faint traces of the black eye and the healing lip, then pointed to her arm. Lian noticed this smallest one was shivering.

"My arm's fine," she said, and took off her jacket to show them. "You are a very good healer. Don't be afraid now." She slipped the white jacket over Poonie's shoulders, and the creature trembled. "It will keep you warmer."

Poonie's neck was too thick for her to fasten the top button so Lian tied the hood strings loosely. Cuddles and Naldo looked downright disapproving. The effect of a human jacket on a lumpie was not becoming to a lumpie. Poonie untied the strings and handed the jacket back to Lian.

"O.K.," said Lian. "I meant well." They all smiled at her, and as if by unspoken agreement, set off together for the halls.

· *11* ·

After the brightness of the morning the hall seemed very dark as she followed the three of them inside. The air smelled of grass and wild mustard, scents she had come to associate with lumpies. Perhaps they slept in here when the night was cold. Hearing a rustling movement, she turned on her pocket torch and gave an "Oh!" of surprise.

In the hallway, assembled as if for a group portrait, was the entire lumpie colony. They posed in a semicircle, smallest seated in front, next size standing, and adults erect in the two back rows. Sixty pairs of big eyes stared as she stood openmouthed.

They weren't frightening even in this number, but disconcerting. She didn't know what, if anything, they expected of her. Maybe they were simply frightened of the noises and were hiding in here.

"I came to look around," she said. They watched her mouth closely as she spoke. "Dr. Farr is going to start working on the dome tomorrow. . . ."

Then she remembered that, as she came down the path, she had been thinking of pictures on these walls, hoping she could find images of grouped lumpies . . . and here were the lumpies, assembled for a picture.

"You *are* telepaths!" she whispered in awe, and felt a wave of helplessness because she could not understand them. Yet they didn't comprehend humans completely; she remembered Billy's offering her the beetle for breakfast. It was as if they understood out of context. Like knowing she wanted to see them in a picture, but not . . .

"Cuddles, I want to see old pictures on the walls." She pointed. "To study them. Come." She set off on the route they had taken yesterday, and the rest followed the V of light from her torch.

She moved slowly, checking every spot on the walls that could possibly be decorative. Finally Cuddles caught her hand, led her into an alcove, and pointed. On the wall, behind layers of dirt and grime, the pocket light revealed a dim group of forms.

"Yes!" She nodded to Cuddles. "Exactly!"

As she removed the tube of liquid soap and the washcloths she had concealed in her jacket, the lumpies gathered around to watch. Ignorant of the medium used and not wanting to damage the picture, she lightly brushed a corner with a rag. Dirt crumbled away. She stepped back to look, then began to work more rapidly. The image was embedded in hard panel. There was a fringe of what looked like filthy fur around it. When she had cleaned less than a third of the picture, the lumpies were crowding behind her, trying to peer over one another's shoulders.

The creatures in the pictures looked like them, but like them as reflected in the most flattering of mirrors. Or idealized by an artist. Larger, more slender, faces bright with intelligence, the subjects were grouped around what appeared to be a model of some sort of machine.

After she had studied the mural for a time, Cuddles took Lian's hand and pulled her away. As he did so, other lumpies picked up dirt from the floor and began to rub it against the picture, covering it up again.

Lian wanted to protest, but she understood why they were doing it. The picture was too revealing. The model was the computer.

She stood there, torn between wanting to shout with joy at this discovery and wanting to cry for these creatures patting dust over their identity. No one would have dared to call the creatures in that picture a name like "lumpie." What had happened to make them afraid—or were they ashamed?—to have others know of their intelligence?

If only they would talk to her. She did not doubt they could, for if they could sing they could talk. But if they talked they might be overheard. It had been almost fifty years since Earth discovered Balthor. Perhaps others had been here before, had in some way terribly harmed them. Or had they been the cause of their own downfall? The computer might be able to tell her.

"There has to be a terminal still operating somewhere in the dome," Lian said. The lumpies went on working. "Maybe I can't talk to you, but part of that computer is still operative. Maybe the library is too. If I can find the buttons that activate it . . . Excuse me."

She set off down the hall, and her three special friends followed. As they hurried along, she flashed the beam from wall to wall. The light revealed what appeared to be directional signs above many doorways. Elsewhere were plaques covered with script.

One wide door opened onto an auditorium full of row upon row of molded yellow seats. She stopped to see if her light would reach the stage. It did not. After a moment Naldo tugged her sleeve as if to say, "Come on."

"Just a minute." She checked the seats; they were designed for smaller lumpie bottoms and backs and stood no more than a foot off the floor. They also showed signs of recent use.

When they reached the end of the corridor, as before, it was Naldo who activated the switch that opened the ramp gate. The camera eyes turned to focus on Lian and her followers. The greeting signal sounded.

Then for no reason Lian understood, the signal stopped. The cameras' lens covers closed. There was much finger signaling and nervous rustling of feet.

When she started down the ramp, Poonie caught her hand and pulled her back.

"It's all right. I'm not going to the computer. I'm going over there." She pointed to the glass panel they had opened the day before. Poonie's grip tightened around her fingers. "It's all right!" Lian said impatiently and pulled free. The lumpie followed her, its eyes troubled. Cuddles came after the two of them.

"Perhaps you're right, Poonie," Lian said as she crossed the floor of the dome. "I don't really know what I'm doing. Maybe it was only luck that I came out of that black hole yesterday. . . ."

There was a scuffling noise behind her. She turned to see Naldo coming at a full run and stopped to wait for him. He swerved past without slowing. By the time Lian saw where he was going and began to chase him, it was too late. He touched the switch and the panel closed as she reached it. Through the window she could see the dials quiver and then jerk upward. Panel lights blinked where nothing had flashed yesterday. It was very strange.

No amount of pleading either by word or thought would make them open anything for her. No switch operated at her touch; she tried them all before giving up the idea of finding a terminal. The dials continued to quiver and jump; there was power, but it wasn't going to help her now. She sighed and turned to go.

As Naldo closed the gate, the other two kept peering into her face. They looked worried, as if afraid they had offended her.

"I'm not angry," Lian told them. "I am thwarted. I wanted to go to Dr. Farr and tell him how you built this place and why you are as you are now. I wanted to . . ."

She fell silent as she realized that part of what she wanted was selfish.

She wanted a discovery of her own as important as the supernova. Like a disappointed child, she had wanted to say to her parents, "I'll show you!"—which was silly, since they had no interest in things like this and wouldn't care much at all.

"My parents are right about one thing," she said aloud. "I need to grow up."

The lumpies smiled at her.

Once outside, they left her almost at once and hurried off into the woods. She had walked nearly half a mile before realizing the jackhammers were silent.

· 12 ·

There was a lot of commotion at the digging site. Long before she could see what was happening, she could hear the crackle of static and shouts of translators on full volume. A slight wind ruffled the leaves and brought the smell of ozone and something else. She paused to sniff— burnt hair? Something with calcium in it, something alive. She began to run.

The entire staff seemed to be down there. They stood in ragged clusters; those at the pit bank did the most shouting; the others surrounded something lying on the grass. She could hear Dr. Farr repeating over and over, "Don't touch them! Don't touch them!"

Scotty was standing apart from the crowd, looking up toward the camp, as if waiting for something. Following her line of sight, Lian saw one of the airtrucks lift off and head toward the dig. It was setting down by the time she was close enough to the linguist to be heard.

"What happened?" she called over the rush of airjets.

"Accident," Scotty answered. "They're going to be flown into the medical center at Limai."

If the medicom couldn't handle it, that meant a severe injury. "Who?"

"Two tolats," Scotty said. "They hit something with the drills. It threw them up there." She sounded incredulous.

There was a break in the crowd, and Lian saw the victims. They lay with their bowl-like bodies resting on top of the sod piles. Their eye stalks dangled; their eight legs hung as limp as chitinous-sheathed legs could hang. What made Lian take a deep breath was the injured tolats' color. Instead of their normal gleaming pink and white, they were a pallid ivory.

"*What* threw them up there?" she asked.

"We think a massive electrical charge, from that." Dr. Scott pointed to the black boxlike building they had been working on. "But we can't get any power reading on it now. We thought they'd cut a power line, but there's no penetration."

"The computer," Lian whispered to herself. "That's why the dials jumped!"

"What? I can't hear you."

"I was just wondering if they were going to be O.K."

"We don't know. Dr. Farr and Tsri Zahr are going with them to Limai. Not that those poor creatures will know they have company."

Lian nodded, not really listening. She was trying to understand how the computer had done this. And if it was deliberate. It must all still be connected, this old city, all the power lines intact. But why would it have defenses like this, against what enemies?

From the airtruck a tank of gas and other apparatus were being rushed over to the injured tolats, and triangular helmetlike sheaths were being fitted over the top end of them. Other tolats and humans were readying a sling device as a stretcher. In a few minutes the victims were hoisted up and carried, legs dangling, into the airtrucks. One of them had regained enough consciousness to try tearing off its oxygen mask. The color on both looked more normal.

"Tolats are a tough breed," said Scotty. She drew a deep breath and pulled her lab coat around her as if chilled. "That was very frightening! We heard this odd crackling noise, and I smelled something hot. They were dancing in blue light, and they still managed to shut off those drills so no one else would get hurt when they let go." The woman blinked rapidly. "I've never liked tolats much. I still don't. But I never saw anyone act with such courage. Once the drills' power went off, the incoming charge really hit them. That's when they flew—"

A silly grin stretched Scotty's mouth and wavered there. Lian saw the woman was either going to cry or go into a fit of laughter as a release from shock.

"Let's go up and get something to drink. Come on." Lian took Scotty's cold hand and tugged as the lumpies did. "There's nothing we can do here. Maybe we can have lunch and then you can show me the lumpies' place. O.K.?"

Scotty nodded, freeing her hand but not trusting herself to speak. The airtruck took off when they were halfway down the road. The woman stopped, turned, and followed it with her eyes until it had disappeared. Lian got the impression she was saying a prayer for the tolats.

To protect the lumpies, Lian felt she had unwittingly subjected this crew to grave danger; if she had told Dr. Farr what she had found yesterday, this accident would not have happened. But she did not regret her decision; it would have happened if she had never come here, and in any event it could not be changed now. There was one bright spot in the situation; no one would doubt her sanity when she told them about the computer.

The dining room quickly became a babble as the rest of the staff arrived to discuss the accident over lunch. The most popular opinion was that either the jackhammers or the cutting torches had somehow built up a charge in the metal. The tolats loudly expressed the opinion that all nonengineers on this expedition were ignorant untranslatables.

But all seemed to agree that this morning's incident was the most interesting discovery they had made to date. They just weren't sure what they had discovered.

It seemed to Lian that ninety-five percent of all this chatter was totally unnecessary and repetitious, that they were all talking in order to avoid thinking about what had really happened, that two of their number had come frighteningly near death in a manner they did not understand. She wondered if that was the source of most social noise —the need to avoid thinking about what really mattered.

"If you're through eating, can we go outside?" she said.

"Noise bothers you, doesn't it?" Scotty guessed later when they were walking along the top of the earthwork en route to the lumpie colony's sleeping place. "Perhaps that's the lumpies' attraction for you—their silence?"

Lian grinned. "Maybe. Maybe lumpies talk only when they have something to say worth hearing."

"Humans can't go by those rules," said Scotty. "Whole weeks would pass in silence." She hesitated, then asked, "Why does noise bother you?"

"It's probably because of the observatory," said Lian. "Everybody works pretty much alone—well, I do anyway. If you talk, it's to the computer—and that's what talks to you. The loudest noise is the wind. For months it's never still."

"Do you have any friends there?"

"Everyone's friendly."

"That's not what I asked."

"No." It bothered Lian to admit that, and she resented having to do so.

"I thought so."

"Why? Am I that unpleasant?"

"Oh, no! You're very nice," Scotty assured her. "But you seem to take solitude for granted. You go off exploring by yourself for hours alone and apparently content. So I guessed you were accustomed to it. I'm not. I have friendly acquaintances here, but no real friends. Loneliness bothers me." She smiled to dismiss the pathos of the remark. "When I left Earth I had no idea what this sort of trip really would be like—how lost it could make you feel to watch your home planet fade in the distance—to see how small Earth is in space. . . ."

"How long will you be here?" asked Lian.

"A year on Balthor, another year in return travel time. It's a working sabbatical for me. And you?"

"I don't know. Until my parents are reassigned, I guess. Or . . ."

"Or what?"

"I decide I want to be assigned someplace else."

They were down at the far end, not far from the entrance to the halls, when Scotty turned off on an angled path that led away from the site. "It's over here someplace. I found it the first day we were surveying."

Unlike the lumpie routes within the site, which followed gentle parabolas, this path meandered into the deep woods, circled massive tree trunks, dipped down along a creek to follow its banks, and then swung uphill.

"Where does this path go?"

Scotty shrugged. "Miles. Going nowhere." She stopped and pointed. "There's a hammock—see it up there?"

Hung from a heavy branch, the hammock fell a yard above ground, too high for a lumpie to climb into without great effort. Lian examined the intricately braided mesh. It was far too beautiful a skill to waste on peeled vines and hang out in the weather. The ground below it bore no tracks, no crushed plants, no signs of wear.

"Have you ever seen them sleep here?" she asked casually.

"No. I've always been here in the daytime. There are more up here."

Scotty forced her way through a thicket, and Lian followed. In the next hour she counted thirty hammocks. None showed any sign of use. Although they had gone to great effort to make it look otherwise, wherever the lumpies slept, it was not here.

· 13 ·

There was a pok-pok game in progress when the airtruck came back in late afternoon. Scotty and Lian were playing mixed doubles with amalfis. Tolats watched from the sidelines.

Pok-pok was one of those rare games that sentient species could play together. It was a mongrel mixture of tennis and amalfi netball. Humans could play in conventional style. The amalfis wore breathing gear to keep from exhausting themselves in this dry atmosphere.

Tolats never played pok-pok or any other game except their own, which was called "Jump!" The smallest tolat could jump ten times its own length and frequently did so.

Since the game was being played on the landing pad, it was interrupted by the airtruck's arrival. Only Dr. Farr and the tolat medic were aboard. It was hard to tell about the tolat, but Dr. Farr looked tired.

"Your colleagues will recover," Dr. Farr told the group that ran to meet them. "They were out of shock when we left. Zizzori has a fractured topshell. Both he and Zarr will need extensive resheathing on their foreclaws and grippers. They were badly scorched. Tsri Zahr is going to stay with them for a day or two until the prosthetic shell is molded."

After Dr. Farr excused himself and went to his quarters to bathe and change, the tolat contingent gathered around the tolat medic to question him further, translators off. The only thing Lian understood was repeated reference to Tsri Farr.

No one felt like resuming the pok-pok game once the crowd broke up. The players went off to take their respective showers. Lian was beginning to get butterflies in her stomach at the thought of telling Dr. Farr about the dome and the lumpies. Her hands were icy as she toweled and dressed. There was no point in putting it off.

Buford was stretched out in the sun in front of Dr. Farr's door when she got there—a band of vivid orange against the gravel. His antennae quivered at her approach, but he did not move. The door was open, and she could hear the man talking; apparently he had a visitor. Not wanting to disturb him or Buford, she was turning away when he called out, "Lian?" and came to the door.

"I—could I talk to you later—privately?"

"Surely. But why not now? I'm just finishing my personal log entry. It'll only take a few minutes more." He saw her look at Buford. "Don't mind our watch worm. Just step over him."

"Do you—like him there?" she said as she made sure her feet cleared the millipede by a wide margin.

"Shhh." His voice lowered to a stage whisper. "Buford's very sensitive. Many staff members don't want him around. He finds this traumatic since he is accustomed to lumpie attention."

"That's what I wanted to talk to you about."

Dr. Farr's eyebrows angled up. "Buford?"

"No. Lumpies. I don't really want to tell you, but I think I have to. Lumpies are—an intelligent species. This city is theirs."

Dr. Farr's expression went blank. He searched her eyes for a moment, then reached over and pulled up a folding chair for her. "You *are* serious?" he said, and when she nodded, "What makes you think so?" As he sat down on the edge of the bed, she saw him turn the log recorder back to "on."

"Shall I begin at the beginning?" she asked for the benefit of the recording.

"I think that would be best."

"Yesterday I was on top of the dome—the center of the eye?—and I heard the same music that I heard before."

He frowned at that but did not interrupt. In fact, he said nothing for the ten minutes it took her to relate the basic story.

When she had finished, Dr. Farr sat there on the bed, still staring at her in expressionless silence. Lian's hyperactive imagination darted in all directions. Was he wondering if she was sane? Angry because she hadn't told him yesterday? In shock?

"You will see that no harm comes to the lumpies?" she said.

At that he stirred and took a deep breath. "Forgive me for sitting here like a lump—" he said. "Poor choice of words—I'm sorry. Of course we'll protect them—if they need it. What I was wondering was if I should tell the others or investigate this myself."

"Oh, I think you'd better tell them," Lian said. "They'll overlook my secretiveness. But yours would be seen as an attempt to gain personal glory."

"I see you are familiar with research personalities," Dr. Farr said. "Behind each dispassionate scientific mask lurks an egomaniac." He paused as another thought occurred, and when he spoke again, his voice had lost some of its customary warmth. "This isn't an elaborate joke, is it, Lian? A hoax on the archaeologists?"

It was her turn to frown. "Why would I do that?"

"We know nothing of each other," he said. "And few jokes seem as enduring as the manufacture of extraordinary cultures for gullible archaeologists and anthropologists to discover. If you knew how many mummies of little green men we are offered, how many fabulous artifacts are carefully manufactured for our benefit. For you to make such an extraordinary find with absolutely no training . . ." He suddenly stopped, and the only sound in the room came from the insects singing in the grass outside. "With no preconceived ideas to blind you"—the words were almost whispered to himself—"no knowledge to be ignored, no innate hostility toward strange animals. . . . I want to see this place before dark!"

Of course they all had to see it immediately. The sun was beginning to make long shadows in the woods. A herd of nalas was feeding on the vines at the edge of the dome. They crashed away into the underbrush, panicked by this parade of chattering strangers.

Although she watched for them, she saw no lumpies anywhere and hoped none were in the old building. None were.

At the entrance to the halls, the staff let her lead the way. She was not sure if their deference was due to politeness, because it was her discovery, or timidity, since with the sun low the entrance looked like a very black cave.

"The ceiling glows a little when the lumpies are in here," she told them.

This caused the tolats to talk excitedly among themselves.

"There will be no bringing lumpies here against their will," Dr. Farr announced, and added with a look at the tolats, "just in case the idea occurred to you."

Only a few had electric torches on their belts, and the inspection tour was cursory. Lian led them perhaps a third of the way in. That took more than an hour because each open door had to be peered into and the unidentified contents discussed. One thing they decided immediately was that this hall had been repeatedly flooded. Those few rooms they could enter were full of soil and vegetable matter from which furniture and other artifacts protruded.

Scotty looked for and found written symbols everywhere. She

greeted each new find with a yell of delight. "I was becoming afraid we'd find nothing," she told Lian, "that I had perhaps wasted three years. But it's wonderful! Marvelous! Intricate! Look at that doorway —see that sign? Isn't it beautiful?" And with that she hugged the girl out of sheer exuberance. "I can hardly wait to get in here tomorrow."

Like the professionals they were, they touched nothing, waiting for the time and tools to examine the site properly without risk of damage through haste. All were pleased and excited by what they saw, especially the artwork on the walls. The dome they would save for tomorrow. If a lumpie could not be persuaded to open the door, the tolats were sure they could bypass the switch.

Oncoming twilight drove them out into the woods again. As they walked back to camp, Lian noticed a subtle change in attitude. Before, almost no one had paid any attention to her. Now, to her great surprise, a *tolat* suggested she be made an honorary member of the expedition. All the other tolats gave their hissing version of three cheers, and the amalfis joined in. "We must sew expedition patches on your jacket sleeves," said Dr. Farr. "You've surely earned them."

But some of the human members of the group, once the first excitement of discovery had passed, seemed resentful and were none too discreet about showing their displeasure. "I find it hard to believe that your find was serendipitous," one man said. "I understand you've been on Balthor quite a while? Long enough to cover a lot of territory?" And a woman said, "I understand you fly alone a lot. This must have been one of your favorite camping places?"

"Why don't they believe I never saw this place until two days ago?" Lian asked Scotty.

"They don't want to," Scotty said. "You have to consider that this expedition includes five renowned extraterrestrial archaeologists. Their grants and their reputations are based on what they find. You arrive, a complete amateur, and two days later announce a major discovery.

You can't expect them all to appreciate your success."

Lian thought that over to see if she should be sympathetic. She decided she wasn't. "I'm not going to publish anything."

Scotty grinned. "Well, in that case," she said, "maybe they'll forgive you someday," and they both laughed.

· **14** ·

From where Lian and the three lumpies sat, the tolats up on the dome looked like crabs dragging push brooms. Actually they were removing vegetation with long-handled vaporizers. Under the vines and a thin layer of soil, the tolats had found the dome was not frosted opaque but a transparent glassy substance.

On the north side a crew was preparing to wash off the glass. The airtrucks had carried up a pump and plastic bags full of water.

At dawn the tolats had rushed to the dome, confident they could get inside. But when they came back for breakfast, they reported they could not activate the gate switch or bypass it. After yesterday's accident there was no question of blasting through. Since the lumpies were nowhere to be found at that hour, the tolats had attacked the problem from the outside.

"Is central unit covered with shield?" one of the engineers had asked Lian at breakfast.

"It's a clear housing. Most of it—" was all she got to say before they started talking among themselves. This dome was exciting them considerably, but they would not say why. That they thought it important was evident by their temporary lack of interest in what lay beneath it.

The rest of the staff was now mapping and photographing the halls and rooms below. Lian would have liked to be with them, but the lumpies created a problem. Like householders when workmen invade the home, the lumpies wanted to see what was going on—so long as Lian was there. The entire colony followed her everywhere she went, which admittedly did make for crowded hallways and difficulty in moving equipment and lighting.

After overhearing several derogatory remarks aimed at the gentle but curious creatures, Lian decided to go outside with them. Lumpies might not understand these languages, but she was almost certain they would pick up the ugly tone in them.

On her way out she was stopped by the photographer, who thanked her for leaving and spoiled it by adding, "To be honest, I—uh—well, some of us are upset by them. I'm sure you understand. They've always been fat dumb animals. Now we have to stop and remember they aren't. They're getting in my way. I mean, they *look* so stupid!"

"They don't!" said Lian, instantly angry. "How would you look gray, bald, a hundred pounds heavier, and naked? Would you like it if I looked at you then and said, 'Wow, a fat dumb animal'?"

"You don't understand," the man said. "I was trying to be polite, to explain—"

"No," said Lian. "You were trying to be forgiven for bigotry."

That exchange and what prompted it was still bothering her an hour later as she sat watching the tolats work. This complete dismissal of the lumpies from the beginning, when they had first been given their name, puzzled her.

Was it because they suggested a human, with their big sad eyes, clown smile, and dumpy figure, that humans laughed at them? And if the humans laughed, then did that give other sentient species the freedom to express chauvinistic disdain for lumpies similar to the contempt they felt for humans but dared not express?

There was a definite comfort in the purity of astrophysics, she thought. There were no emotional elements. She suddenly understood more her parents' passion for their work. It shut out things like this . . . it shut out the problems of normal life. And some of the joy.

Cuddles touched her shoulder and, when she glanced up, patted her cheek comfortingly and then pointed toward the dome. The push broom crew had finished, and the second crew had started the pump. A hose had been rigged in the already cleaned center so that water sprayed up like the horn of a trumpet and fell, to flush down the surface of the dome. That the water made the surface slick was obvious by the way the workers began to slide off it.

The airtrucks droned back and forth with dripping water bags hanging from the hoists on both ends. Slowly red soil darkened to wet mud, then to a thick liquid that gravity flowed downward. The glassy surface below began to shine through. It appeared almost black and reflected the rainbows dancing in the spray overhead.

Cuddles and Poonie were having a long conversation, evidently discussing the dome, since they kept nodding in its direction. They got up, walked through the wet grass and mud, and tried to peer in. From past experience Lian suspected this was one-way glass—that one could see out of the dome but not into it. They touched the surface several times and appeared to be taking its temperature.

"I wonder," said Lian, and got to her feet. "Does that absorb radiation? Is that what powers the energy cells . . . or part of them?" That would explain the tolats' interest. If the computer was still working, there had to be some reason why it was still working. If they got electrocuted, again there had to be a reason. She joined the lumpies at dome's edge; the wet surface was icy cold.

Seeing her there, one of the tolats called, "It is (untranslatable). It could pass through star fire and not heat."

"But what is it?" she called back.

Whatever the tolat said consumed at least twenty sounds in its language. The translator converted his answer to "Beautiful!"

An airtruck lumbered in to land. As it sank down to unhook the heavy water bags, one struck a tree and ripped. The water dropped in one great splash upon the tolat, knocking him flat on his back.

Thrown off balance by the weight of the remaining water bag, the airtruck flipped up, came down hard on the weighted side, teetered precariously, and safely set down.

The whole incident took less than ten seconds. Poonie galloped toward the half-drowned tolat. Lian and the others followed. Lian was running, not to help the tolat, but because she was afraid that if Poonie touched the creature, its heavy claw arms would strike out in fear and hurt Poonie. Pausing to peer at the fallen tolat, Poonie looked like a small gray bear with an extra pair of arms. The tolat crew crouched to jump on Poonie. "Don't," yelled Lian. "He's a medic! Don't hurt him." And the tolats paused.

Poonie waved to the other two. They hurried around the still body and lifted it by the opposite side of the shell. Poonie splayed his fingers against the bottom shell, braced himself, and nodded. The other two gave the victim one quick bounce. There was a gurgling noise, and water poured out of the tolat's mouth. Its legs jerked convulsively as Poonie shoved. More water came, and a loud hissing word. Poonie nodded and backed away; his helpers lowered the body.

With a grunt the wet tolat flipped itself over, eyes whipped up to stare at the lumpies; then it pivoted on its toes, said to its kind, "Engineers!", and scuttled back to work. From a tolat there was no higher praise.

Within the dome, control boards were lighting in a dozen auxiliary rooms; inactive terminals hummed to life as the power cells charged with sunlight. Here and there was a dry, twiglike snapping of ancient circuitry shorting out. In the dense liquid honeycomb beneath the blue floor thought flickered from cell to cell. The mind that was the Counter began to revive from its prolonged malnourishment and consider thoughts of survival other than its own.

In its weakened condition, to repel yesterday's attack on its outer hull had almost cost it its life. It remembered the alien Guardian coming in with the people; then pain had taken away all other awareness. Now it was alone again. The Counter called out to the people.

· 15 ·

The lumpies were listening to something. Their faces had the rapt look of a cat watching invisibles. An airtruck came in to land. They paid no attention to it.

"Can you hear anything?" Lian called to the tolats. Their eyes went up. "It would be coming from the dome."

"Signals? Sounds?" They advanced at once and touched the glass with their foreclaws, feeling for vibrations. "No sound," came the report. One hurried off for an instrument of some sort and brought it over to the dome. After a few seconds the tolat gave an oddly joyous jump. "Cells charge!" it hissed jubilantly. "Cells charge!"

Oblivious to this, first Cuddles, then Poonie dropped to their feet and started off. The rest followed. Then, as if remembering something, Cuddles circled back and held out a hand to Lian. Seeing her leave with the lumpies, the tolats began gathering their equipment, preparing to follow.

The vines around the entrance had all been stripped away. The bank below was trampled flat and littered with equipment. The round door, too heavy to move, lay where she had first seen it. The air of peace was gone and the change saddened her. Lights had been strung in the halls. Staff members looked up in surprise as this procession of lumpies and tolats hurried by. One by one the archaeologists put down their work and came along.

As the gate slid up to reveal the interior of the dome, there was an excited hiss from the tolats and a soft "Wow!" from Lian. The polished roof turned the sky to pale green, the clouds deeper green, and trees fringed it all. The tolats barely glanced up before pushing past Lian and lumpies to hurry down the ramp. They circled the floor, their legs clacking as they jumped to see into each cubicle, where panels now glowed with light. Slowly the rest of the staff straggled in and joined the tolats in their exploration.

"Be careful of the open end of the computer," Lian warned them, and then remembered to whistle the response that shut off the bell tone.

"Which part?" said Dr. Farr.

"The far end."

A tolat made a hissing sound that could have been contempt. "This is all computer. That"—it pointed to the central unit—"in there"—it pointed to the cubicles lining the dome—"floor, roof, walls . . . all one artificial mind. We think. Yes."

There was a blast of static that made Lian jump, a high-frequency whine, and thumping noises. The lumpies huddled together nervously, and everyone else froze where they were, not knowing what to expect. From the central speaker came a sound like a child chanting verse, swift and melodic; then the voice slowed and went lower in pitch and became almost a song. Several of the lumpies rose to listen, faces alert. There was nervous laughter from the humans.

"Be quiet!" Dr. Farr commanded. "Listen. It's speaking a language."

"Lis-son," the computer's voice slowly mimicked, and the intruders backed away from it.

The faintest of screeches came from the computer. A panel was sliding open on its blank side to reveal a large display screen flickering to life. A spectrum of color bands crossed it in horizontal drift. Script flashed on the screen and was made jumpy by glitches. A melodic sound track came on at a very low volume.

The script dissolved to dark mist, and out of the mist came the picture of a solar system, its star much too red. Almost immediately the picture changed to something totally foreign—a geometric array of what could be dancing mold spores or flowers. But if it made no sense to Lian or the staff, it did to the lumpies. Either the picture or the sounds she had been dismissing as background music were pulling them closer to the screen. They clustered around her, sitting on the floor to watch.

After a moment Lian joined them and tried to clear her mind to truly hear, but there was too much distraction in the room. The tolats had gathered in a hissing clump. Several were recording this film. Some staff members were still exploring the walls, tapping the panels, trying to force them open. The lumpies paid attention only to the screen.

Since the rest of the film was unintelligible to all but the lumpies, what was the point of that opening shot? Lian wondered. Was it an acknowledgment of her and her interests, a gift from this mind to hers, like giving beetles to Buford?

As if in response to her thought, the screen went blank, flickered, and then repeated the prologue shot of the dying star. The camera closed in on the ninth planet to show an encapsulated history of that world and of its people. They saw the ancestors of the lumpies first as the creators, then the stewards, and finally the pampered wards of a technology so advanced that it could attempt to perpetuate both itself and its creators by assembling, over generations, a vast fleet of ships that left the orbit of their planet and, one by one, like great searching eyes, disappeared into the darkness of space.

When the pictures again became abstract forms, there was restless movement and whispering among the research group. Then a tolat gave voice to the obvious. "This site is not city. It is starship. We are standing on control deck."

· 𝟣𝟨 ·

From their dust bath by the landing pad, wortles watched the shining
aircar sit down. The hatch opened immediately, and the pilot stepped
out—a tall woman in white wearing dark glasses like a mask. Just as her
toe touched the ground, Buford hurried across the tarmac to meet
her.

The pilot retracted the toe and from the bottom step called, "Hello?
Is anyone here?" The worm's antennae quivered. Both pilot and craft
had the thin, cold scent of high altitudes where no bugs sang. Like the
wortles, the worm immediately lost interest.

When she saw the orange thing disappear into the tall grass, the pilot
stepped down. "Hello?" she called again. Her tone suggested a voice
accustomed to immediate response. When none came, she strode up
the main street, boots flashing in the sunlight.

A tolat who had been repairing the autoserver came out of the dining
hall and stopped still, as surprised to see the visitor as she was to see
it.

"You are a tolat!" There was relief in identification.

"You are human. Yes." The tolat walked over to stare at the large
blue aircar, finding it of greater interest than its pilot.

"I'm looking for my daughter. Is she here?"

The word "daughter" meant nothing to the androgenous tolat. The words "Mount Balthor Observatory" on the side of the car did.

"Star watcher is with Tsri Farr."

"And where would that be?"

The tolat pointed a gripper arm at the dig. "Down there."

The woman glanced at the distance between herself and the site. "Would you call them, please?"

"They are inside. Where intercom does not operate. Walk down." The pragmatic tolat returned to its work. It had answered all questions necessary.

This woman who thought nothing of traveling across light years of space in a metal container disliked the idea of walking alone on this planet's surface. It made her feel vulnerable to be exposed to this bowl of open sky and to living creatures. If it were not for Lian . . . She began to walk.

Lian hardly heard the tolat or the outburst of conversation that followed; she was absorbed in the feeling emanating from the lumpies. It was as if they had received some understanding that caused their minds to clear and lighten, as if hope had freed them at last from some long and onerous burden.

They sat as they had before, silently watching the screen that continued to show something intelligible only to themselves, but now their eyes glowed, the smiles were true smiles, and their faces began to resemble their ancestors.

She looked from their faces to those of the staff around them, outsiders, excited by the same discovery, but in a totally different way —and almost totally ignoring each other.

"Can you imagine bringing this thing in for a landing?" she heard Dr. Farr say. "That's no earthwork; it's the dirt the landing jets blew up when it came down!"

"It may be resting on a crater it dug."

"How much flood damage do you think there is?"

"The weight of it must have depressed the ground by . . ."

"How far down do you think the levels go?"

"Lian?" Dr. Farr touched her shoulder. "Did you recognize their solar system? Could they have come from the star in supernova?"

"Has this ship been here at least a hundred thousand years?" she asked.

He shook his head. "Probably no more than three hundred at the most."

She grinned. "That's hardly a wink of time's eye. No, they aren't from the supernova. The size and heat of that sun would have killed life on any planet circling it long, long ago. If the lumpies' star novas, you and I will never see it—even if we learn which system it is."

"It takes so long?"

"In human time, yes. In sidereal time it's very fast."

He mused over this for a moment. "So when I say, as an archaeologist, that a culture is very old, my concept of great antiquity is an astrophysicist's concept of 'only a moment ago'?"

"Something like that," she agreed. "It takes a little getting used to—" She paused in midsentence, distracted by the movement of a human figure standing outside, looking down at the edge of the dome. As Dr. Farr watched, all animation left Lian's face and it became as blandly expressionless as a lumpie's. "It's my mother," she said, answering the question he had not yet spoken aloud.

"Here?"

"Out there." She indicated direction with a lift of her chin, thinking, Why did she have to come now and spoil this?

"Handsome woman," was Dr. Farr's first verbal reaction. "Why didn't she call and give us warning? It would have saved her from having to hunt us up down here."

"It would never occur to her to call," Lian said. "I'd better go meet her. She looks lost."

"I'll go with you." Dr. Farr glanced about, his face showing his fear that they might miss something important while they were gone.

"You don't have to."

"Oh, but I do, Lian," he said with a smile. "First because she's important to you—and also because the further one goes from civilization, the more important courtesy becomes."

"Visitor outside," someone called.

"It's Dr. Webster—from the observatory," Dr. Farr answered as a general announcement. Heads turned to see the visitor through the green glass dome, then turned to look at Lian.

Poonie looked away from the screen to Lian's face, then got up and walked over to see. Cuddles followed, and they watched the stranger circling the rim of the dome above them. One by one the other lumpies noticed, and there was much finger talking among them.

"You're not going to leave us?" Scotty said as she caught up to Lian and Dr. Farr at the ramp. "You're not going home now?"

"I . . . I suppose I am." Lian felt a sudden sharp sense of loss. Her mother's appearance was so unexpected an intrusion in the midst of the morning's excitement that she had not truly absorbed its meaning until now. "I guess so," she repeated numbly.

Dr. Farr looked equally surprised by the idea. "I hadn't thought of that," he admitted. "How stupid of me. Of course that's why she's here . . . why you look so . . . it's not a courtesy call."

"No," said Lian. "Well, maybe in a sense. Otherwise they would have sent Max to get me."

"Oh?" said the man, but Lian hurried off without an explanation.

· 17 ·

Lian was a good fifty yards ahead of Dr. Farr and Scotty when she caught sight of her mother standing alone at the edge of the meadow. Perhaps it was the woman's look of indecision, or the fact that she appeared physically diminished by the wild, that dissolved Lian's resentment. She called a glad hello and ran up the slope to meet her.

Dr. Webster submitted to the exuberant hug, but Lian could feel the woman's body tighten as if there were a steel armature supporting that softness. The embrace was not quite returned; instead her mother lightly gripped Lian's arms, which made stepping away easier, more graceful, and the girl's clutch seem gauche. Dr. Webster was, her child would realize in years to come, an unconscious expert in the art of inflicting small disappointments.

"You look well—except for that"—her finger not quite touched the nearly healed lip—"and a general state of grime."

Lian could see her own reflection in the sunglasses her mother wore. There were smudges on her face and clothing from being in the dome. Reduced to the ranks of childhood for the first time since coming here, she automatically began brushing off.

"Your father and I were shocked when we saw the mechanic's

on-screen report from the hangar at Limai. I'm relieved to see you are safe. The aircar is almost a total wreck."

"I'm sorry." Lian apologized for the loss of the expensive car as automatically as she had brushed off her clothing. And for the same reasons.

"I was lucky," she said, "in more ways than one." Her face lit up as she remembered. "Do you know what we've found?"

"You must see the supernova, Lian." Dr. Webster smiled to soften her dismissal of youthful enthusiasms for the unimportant. "That's why I came. It's quite an extraordinary experience to see the death of a massive star in so spectacular an explosion. We had never seen a supernova before, Ben and I, only remnants of the blast. To see it bloom from a dull red ball into ever-expanding brilliance—"

For want of a better focal point, Lian was still watching her reflection in the left lens of Dr. Webster's glasses, one part of her mind listening, another aware of a sense of unreality. Why had she apologized for wrecking the car? Things that needed feeling were not being felt; things that needed saying were not being said. They were going to be ignored again. Yet they were as real as starlight.

Some old patience snapped in her and she cried out, "Mother, I nearly died! Can't you picture that? Can't you let that be real to you for just a moment?"

In the human silence a bird sang a liquid song. Lian would remember that sound, that stillness broken by her mother's voice. "Yes, I can. And I have. But you did not die. That is the reality. For me to experience your fear would be an exercise in voyeurism—which would in no way alter what happened to you."

"But don't you feel anything?" said Lian, who did not understand.

Dr. Webster took a deep breath. When she spoke, her voice was reasoned, distant. "If I felt nothing, I wouldn't be here, feeling awkward, not knowing how to comfort you."

Without quite believing, but wanting to, Lian impulsively reached out, and her mother eluded a second embrace by catching the girl's wrists and holding them "Touch does not cross the barrier. Besides, we have an audience,' Dr. Webster murmured. "We can discuss this later on the way home."

In honor of the approaching strangers, she flipped up her glasses. Her face wore its public mask. Lian made the necessary introductions.

"Thank you both for your help and kindness to Lian," said Dr. Webster, "and for arranging for the car's salvage. We will, of course, reimburse your expedition for all expenses you've incurred, Dr. Farr, and replace any clothing or supplies Lian has used."

"That's not necessary," he said, "but we would like one favor, a very large one—if Lian agrees. We would like to keep her with us for a time. She's made a great discovery here, and we need her help to take full advantage of it."

"Do you mean it?" Lian said before Dr. Webster could speak. "You'd like me to stay?"

"Very much!" Dr. Farr assured her. "We need your help, your good mind, your rapport with the lumpies—"

"Because of Lian we've accomplished more in two days than we had in the previous six weeks," Scotty explained to Dr. Webster. "Heaven knows we need her if we're going to get any cooperation from the lumpies. They trust her. Not us."

"I wonder why that is," Dr. Farr said thoughtfully and frowned. "We haven't harmed them at all. Have we?"

"No. We've either ignored them or condescended to be amused by them. But Lian looks on them as interesting equals. If you were a sentient alien, to which attitude would you respond?"

"The latter—even if I were human." Dr. Farr laughed at his own joke.

"I think your remaining here is out of the question," Dr. Webster said to Lian after listening to this exchange. "Your training doesn't equip you for this sort of work. And if you've been controlling the animals by making pets of them, surely the same effect could be achieved with tranquilizers. I'm sure that sort of thing is available at Limai—"

"You don't understand," Dr. Farr said. "Hasn't Lian told you?"

"I started to—"

"But we didn't have much time to talk." Dr. Webster glanced at her watch. "It will be nearly dark by the time we get back."

Lian took a deep breath and plunged. "I'm not going back with you today." She had not planned to say that, but once it was said, she felt a great weight roll off her chest. "I think I want to stay here if I can —for a little while—anyhow." It was her first major defiance of authority, and it was scary. "You'll understand when I explain."

Two small white lines appeared at the corners of Dr. Webster's mouth. Surprise, anger, and confusion flickered around her eyes before she could control that self-betrayal. For a long moment she studied Lian with almost clinical appraisal, then turned to Dr. Farr and Dr. Scott.

"This is something Lian and I must discuss privately. If she will walk with me to my car, I won't take any more of your time."

After proper good-byes were said, the archaeologists watched the other two walk away; Lian earnestly talking, explaining; Dr. Webster listening without comment.

Where the path curved and trees threatened to obscure the view, Lian turned and waved. She meant the wave to reassure them of her return and interpreted their worried expressions as a compliment. "So you see," she told her mother, "we've just begun to understand what happened to the lumpies and why. I'm the first person they've trusted. If I leave now, they won't have a friend. They—"

"But they are not your responsibility," said Dr. Webster. "In no way does astrophysics qualify you to do social work among regressed aliens. What can you possibly do for them?"

"Understand them. Interpret until we can break their language codes on the computer—"

"You speak their language?" The sunglasses stared at Lian.

"No. . . ." Lian hesitated, knowing what her mother's reaction would be. "They are telepaths and I—we can understand each other sometimes."

"You are now a telepath?"

"No . . . yes, a little."

"I see."

"I am not ill, Mother, and I didn't hit my head in the crash. Dr. Scott suspected them of being telepathic long before I came."

"Then why didn't they trust her?"

"I don't know," she said.

"Nor do I." They walked in uncomfortable silence for a time; then, "I don't know what's prompted all this, Lian. Possibly it's an effect of trauma from your accident. The thought of our own death, even when that thought is repressed, does strange things to the mind. But I suspect you are still young enough to be immune from that. I do think it has something to do with your age, with your tendency to be emotional. I don't remember being fourteen—"

"I'm almost sixteen."

"Whatever. But I remember always knowing what I was, what I wanted to be. You have chosen to be an astrophysicist—"

Maybe it was the wrong choice, Lian thought, wondering if a decision made at nine locked her forever into an observatory.

When Lian did not respond, Dr. Webster started to speak, shook her head, as if thinking it would be useless, then decided to try anyhow. "Have you considered this situation objectively?" she said. "Have you considered what the outcome of your involvement might be? You feel compassion for these creatures—and that is commendable. But it could also be very destructive to you. Suppose you find malnutrition has made them as simple as they are reputed to be? There are few things more heartbreaking than an endearing idiot. If wealth of any form exists in that ruin, they may become the victims of whoever tries to take it from them. Historically, lost tribes have had tragic endings once so-called civilized man found them. The same potential for tragedy exists here."

Lian knew from past experience that, given the chance, her parents could convince her of almost anything—and with sound, logical reasoning. She also knew she wanted to stay here and that if she listened too closely to her mother, she would capitulate and go with her. And so she did not listen.

When Dr. Webster finished speaking, the uncomfortable silence returned. The woman admitted defeat. "Perhaps this current interest of yours will soon lose its charm," she said. "I suspect it will. Possibly it will have educational value. More than I would like it to have."

They were within sight of the camp now. The familiar blue executive aircar flashed in the sun, and somehow this gleaming reminder of home made Lian feel guilty. Her mother stopped and turned to her. "I can find my way from here," she said. "To keep our records straight, as an aspiring doctoral candidate employed by the observatory, you have several vacation days earned. Or perhaps we should count this as sick leave." With what could have been shyness, she reached out and patted Lian's cheek, her fingers cool and dry. "I'll keep in touch," she said, and left. She did not look back or wave.

Lian was halfway back to the dome when she heard the aircar lift off. She looked back to see it rise at full power, swing toward the north like a compass needle, and shoot away over the mountains. The trees around the camp lashed in the jet wind.

The girl grinned in spite of her mood. She had made her mother angry, and the car was suffering for it. "Poor car," she said.

Anger hit the Counter's sensors like static. Narration paused. Glitches marred the viewing screen for several seconds while the Counter analyzed this remarkable energy burst. The Guardian was aware of it, yet did not seem frightened by it. The Counter was impressed. Perhaps such energy could be used. The angry mind receded in the distance, and the static faded.

· *18* ·

As she stood watching the aircraft become a speck in the sky, leaves rustled and Poonie appeared. Immediately behind came Naldo and Cuddles. All three looked very pleased . . . and something else, Lian thought.

"Did you follow me?" There was some hesitation, and then to her delight Poonie nodded "yes," as a human would. "You were afraid I was leaving?" Again came the nod. "What would you have done if I had?" she asked and in response saw tears form in Poonie's eyes and spill down the gray cheeks.

This mute grief made sympathetic tears well in her own eyes before she could stop them. "But I can't stay with you forever," she said. "Only for now. Only until . . ."

But the lumpies wanted to hear none of that, even if they truly understood what she was saying. They gently grabbed hold of her hands and tugged, impatient to get back to the dome.

When they walked in, the big display screen was still holding an audience of lumpies and tolats enthralled (the lumpies because they understood it, the tolats because they did not). Only Dr. Farr and Scotty remained of the humans.

"You're back!" Dr. Farr's smile exposed both gums. "I'm so glad!"

"What was your mother's reaction to all this?" Dr. Scott's eyes searched Lian's face.

"She—I'm on vacation or sick leave," said Lian, and saw Scotty's face assume a noncommittal expression.

"Oh," was all Scotty said.

"Where did the others go?"

"The novelty of this film wore off, and they went to explore what they can of the ship. So quickly we become bored with wonder and search for new wonder." Dr. Farr sighed. "It is getting a bit tedious."

"I passed the photographer and another man on the meadow. Where do you think they were headed?" said Lian.

"Vincent? Maybe after another camera. I don't know."

"Or to the videocom to be the first to report the discovery and take credit for the story?"

"Oh, they wouldn't do that—" His eyes locked on hers. "We'd have half of Limai here by dawn! Every fortune hunter—" He turned and looked over the group. "Zorn? May I talk to you a minute?"

The tolat scurried over.

Dr. Farr led them a discreet distance away from the others and explained the situation. "If anyone talks to Limai and tells outsiders we have a starship here, we may attract visitors we can't handle. People might be hurt."

"This is probable," agreed the tolat, and added, "We will fix videocom. Also airtrucks. Isolate camp."

"Can you do it before those men get there?" said Lian.

"Can tolats jump?" replied Zorn, and left them. They watched him hissing to several of his people, and then four tolats hurried from the dome.

"What made you think of that so quickly?" Dr. Farr asked as they walked back to where they could see the screen.

Lian shrugged. "I guess I've been worrying about what would happen to the lumpies ever since I suspected this place was theirs."

"Speaking of the lumpies, is it my imagination or do they look somehow different?" he asked.

Lian studied them for a moment. "Their faces have expression now," she said. "They aren't pretending. . . ." She faltered for lack of words to explain it. "Suppose you had to pretend to be stupid to survive—so that you didn't threaten anyone who could hurt you. What sort of look would you wear on your face?"

Dr. Farr immediately crossed his eyes and let his jaw hang slack. "Perhaps drool a bit," he added.

"You couldn't keep up that pose for long," said Scotty as she joined them. "If you were intelligent, you'd do what the lumpies do—dead-pan."

"But *why* did they do it?" the man persisted. "They had the technology here to sustain them on arrival, give them time to acclimate before moving out. Yet they built nothing, did nothing. I don't understand it."

"I think we'll find out soon," said Lian. "The computer is talking to them. Whatever it's saying . . ."

Like a person long deprived of fellowship, the Counter could not stop talking once it started. There was so much to tell, so long a time to make up for, so many things it wanted its people to know. With each passing hour of sunlight, the Counter thought of more and more information it needed to impart.

One by one the smallest lumpies fell asleep on their feet, arms folded over their chests, heads resting on the legs or side of whoever was nearest to them. Some of the adults were staring too fixedly at the screen. Lian checked her watch. More than three hours had passed since the film began. No wonder they were glassy-eyed.

She tried to pay attention, but her mind was wandering. What was going to happen to the lumpies? Why did her mother make her feel as if she were six years old sometimes? This dome was much too dirty to house a computer; there was a haze in the still air. Dust motes danced in the light cone focused on the computer housing. And it was too hot in here. Lian opened her jacket, unsnapped the cuffs, and yawned. There was a camera watching her; she stared up at it, thinking, Why don't you take a break so we can all go and eat?

The Guardian was turning off; the Counter could not pinpoint why. The Guardian's thought processes seemed almost totally occupied by images of airborne particles and edibles. The Counter's own people were similarly preoccupied. The Counter fell quiet to reflect on this new input. With one minute portion of its mind it tested long-unused connections and found them responding.

To its great surprise, no sooner had the Counter stopped talking than its entire audience rose to leave. In less than two minutes the dome was empty, the gate closed. The Counter was alone again. It thought it over. In human terms its analysis could have been summarized as, "It must have been something I said."

· 19 ·

Like children released from school, the lumpies ran out into the sunshine. Although they didn't seem to be talking, their eyes, their smiles, their very gait gave the impression of ebullience. By the time Lian, Scotty, and Dr. Farr reached the outer door, the last of the lumpies could be seen romping up the earthwork and down into the thick woods on the other side.

"Do you think we could follow them?" asked Scotty. "They look so happy . . . as if they were going off to celebrate." She looked rather wistful.

"I don't think it would be polite," Dr. Farr said.

"Probably not," she agreed with a sigh. "We don't know their customs. They might feel we were intruding on a family gathering."

"I think they're just hungry and went to find lunch," said Lian.

"Something so mundane?" asked Dr. Farr.

Lian returned his grin, then looked at the door. "I don't feel like going back inside today. I spend almost all my time indoors at home."

"At your age? Why?" Dr. Farr obviously did not approve.

"Because we're up most nights working, and we sleep during the day. Besides, there's no place to go. Just a road between the telescope domes. Half the time the weather is too cold to go out." By mutual unspoken consent, they began walking back to camp.

"But you're so close to the best climate on Balthor," the man said. "Don't you ever go on vacation? Perhaps fly to the coast, or down here? We've been here only six weeks, and I know a dozen scenic places where you could camp."

"No," said Lian, and seeing him frown, explained. "Most of our staff, and my parents, too, prefer being indoors. They come from cities or colonies; they've spent most of their lives on spaceships or observation satellites. Always enclosed. Large open space frightens them. Insects and animals terrify them; they think everything is going to bite. They like walls around them and floors below, rooms preferably carpeted and climate-controlled. They are children of the Container Generation."

The man gave her an appraising look. "You've observed all this? Or did they tell you how they feel?"

"No one admits things like that. They don't even think about them."

"But you do?"

"I get very restless. That's why I make the supply runs, just for an excuse to get outside, to get away, to see trees and water. Limai isn't scenic, but at least—"

"It's a change of scene?" he said, and frowned thoughtfully. "Your parents, Lian—what do they plan for you? What was their purpose—"

"What was that?" Scotty raised her hand for quiet. From somewhere deep in the woods came a cascade of sounds. They stopped and held their breath to listen, and the sound came again. "It appears to be a song."

"Or lumpies talking," whispered Lian. "Listen to the short phrases. The computer must have convinced them it was safe to talk."

"Do you think so?" Scotty's eyes lit up. "Let's see if we can find them? We don't have to intrude. We could stay hidden and watch."

"You must excuse me," whispered Dr. Farr. "I must get back to camp to call Tsri Zahr," and he left them with a wave. Scotty and Lian hardly saw him go.

It was like following elusive birds through the woods. Either the lumpies didn't want to be seen or their voices carried much farther than was normal. A flute-like call would sound, seemingly from behind the next bush. It would be answered by a warble from a nearby tree. But when they reached the tree, there was no one there. For large creatures, they moved with great stealth. No snapping twigs or rustling leaves betrayed them. They left no tracks the two humans could read.

They followed for twenty minutes or more, always within earshot but never sighting them. The farther they got from the site, the more the character of the forest changed. Thicket, vines, and second growth gave way to larger and larger trees, spaced in almost parklike order with enough sunlight to allow grass to grow beneath the leaf canopy.

Lian temporarily lost interest in the chase. "Does this look natural to you," she asked, "the way these trees are growing?"

"I hadn't noticed. Actually I don't know much about trees. How should they grow?"

"At random. Not in arrangements. Not all the same kind. I think this is an orchard."

"If the lumpies planted it, then they haven't totally regressed," Scotty said vaguely. "I wonder what kind of trees they are." Her main attention was still on the distant voices.

Lian shook her head; she didn't know. The trunks were thick, the leaves broad and shiny. As she walked, staring up at the branches, she stepped on something hard. Thinking it was a stone, she ignored it, only to step on another and trip, falling onto the grass. She rubbed her ankle and reached for the offending stone, wanting to throw it with that same illogic that makes a person kick a chair after stubbing a toe.

The object her hand closed over was not a stone but a green gourdlike fruit.

Dr. Scott hurried over and knelt beside her. "Are you hurt?" Lian shook her head and handed her the fruit.

"I've seen the lumpies eating these, but they were yellow," Scotty said, and detached a small sheathed knife from her belt.

Once through the outer rind, it was like cutting bread dough; the fruit split with reluctance to reveal a pale gold interior and five brown seeds. Lian took the half offered for examination. Where her fingers gripped, the fruit crushed to juice. The odor was winy, vaguely sickening with fermentation.

"I think these are windfalls," Lian said. The word "windfalls" evoked a memory, and for a moment she was in an orchard on Earth, smelling the scent of ripe peaches, feeling the warmth of Earth's sun on August-bare skin.

Dr. Scott had risen and wandered over to the nearest tree, where she found several yellowish fruit and picked them. Lian saw her cut one open and comment on it without really hearing what she said.

"Lian?" Scotty was holding a chunk of fruit on the knife blade.

"What?"

"This is more like the fruit I saw the lumpies eating, and . . ."

"De leep," said someone so close by that they both started. A small lumpie was standing behind them. "De leep," it said again. It stood erect and reached between them. Its little gray fingers closed deftly over the chunk, slid it off the blade, and popped it into its mouth. Then with both hands it took the whole fruit from Dr. Scott and walked off. As they watched the lumpie go, Cuddles, Poonie, and Naldo walked into view partway down the orchard and stood watching them.

"It was hungry," said Lian, and laughed to see the infant march away.

"It talked!" Scotty said. "It talked to us! Maybe the others will talk now."

"Maybe . . ." said Lian, trying to remember what it was she had known while in the black hole of their computer. She suddenly glanced down to see a large gray beetle positioning itself to feed on the rotten fruit they had tossed aside. Her lip curled in disgust, and she stepped away. At that Scotty noticed it and gave a little "ugh!" of alarm. From the lumpies came a trill of sounds, and Cuddles came running.

The lumpie looked at the beetle-crowned fruit and then at Lian with an expression of puzzlement, as if to say, "*This* bothered you?" To illustrate the commonplace quality of beetles, he pointed to several more of the insects plowing about among the windfalls.

"I really don't care for beetles," Lian said sheepishly, "especially so close to me."

Cuddles smiled, shook his head in an almost human gesture, said something that sounded like "orakani saroo," and hurried off to rejoin his friends.

"He said, 'They're only fruit bugs.' " Lian frowned. "But not because I understand the words. I just know . . . from the computer. . . ."

"How could you know that?" Scotty paused to think. "There's something about that computer you haven't told us, isn't there? I wondered why it conveniently showed us where they came from—and that was the only thing it showed us that we could understand. . . ." When Lian didn't answer right away, the woman said, "O.K. But if it can do what I suspect now it can, if it can scan our minds . . . that's frightening."

"Not unless someone plans to harm it," said Lian, and then half-grinned. "You're the one who hinted the first day I was here that lumpies might be telepathic."

"And their ancestors built the computer—" Scotty shivered and rubbed the goose bumps that rose on her arms. "I don't want to think too much about that now. Let's go find the tolats and see how they're doing on translating."

The three lumpies looked at one another as the humans left the orchard. There was a brief exchange of ideas; their decision was shared with the rest of the family to let them know where the three were going. As an afterthought, Naldo added the location and solitary status of Payta minor, still eating fruit. Then they set off to find the tolats with the recording devices.

En route they discussed how strange it was that the appearance of the beetles revolted Lian-Guardian when the appearance of the tolats was so much more frightening.

· 20 ·

It was that quiet time of day between work's end and dinner when the staff was occupied with naps or laundry or other personal matters. Lian had spent part of the afternoon watching the tolats strip all the grass and soil off the meadow to expose a section of hull made of a substance that appeared to swallow light. It looked and felt like black jade, oily-smooth. For all its luster, it gave back no reflection.

"Gray people's solar cell," a tolat had said in answer to her question. "Computer may work everything if we give it light again. Perhaps ship's whole skin absorbs energy." From the amount of equipment they were using, Lian suspected the tolats were going to try to unearth most of the ship.

The rest of the time she had spent with Scotty, listening to the recording of the lumpie computer sound track. She had understood none of it and finally gave up to go outside and sit beneath a big tree on the bluff that overlooked the river. The water below was very blue in this light. Hills stretched to the horizon and beyond. Somewhere in the trees a bird was singing. The sound seemed to accent the peacefulness.

"Tsri Lian?" Startled, she glanced up to find herself face to face with a tolat, close enough to see its mouth filaments. As she stared into the cavity, the tolat stared back, eyes up. "Too close," it decided, toe-danced sideways, and lowered its eyes into their slots with a neat little click.

"Three gray people," said the tolat, getting right to the point, "came to us this afternoon. They verbalized for one hundred sixty-three minutes, thirty-one seconds. At our feeding time we stopped to collect equipment. We put recorders down. They took one recorder and ran away with it."

"That's wonderful!"

"No. Our computer cannot analyze language if language is in recorder and recorder is with—"

"I understand that," said Lian, "but they will bring it back, I'm sure."

"Why?"

"Because they understand we need to translate."

"Yes?"

"Yes."

The tolat did not reply, but neither did it go away. She studied the pattern of pink and blue freckles around its eyes and bottom shell so she could recognize it again. She had to assume it was thinking; there was no facial expression to be read. It was. "You believe gray people are still intelligent?"

"Yes."

"They can understand their computer?"

"Yes."

"They will give us adequate verbal samples?"

"I think they will try to."

"Good."

The tolat, having said all it had come to say, walked off. If it had been a human, she would have found its action very rude. As it was, she merely smiled. At least the tolats were interested in the lumpies' intelligence, whatever the motive.

She leaned back against the tree trunk, head cushioned on her hands, and looked up through the leaves to where the nova was the evening star, its blue-and-white dazzle highly visible before the sunset. Her only thought at seeing it was that it was quite beautiful. For the first time since leaving Earth, she was aware of being happy.

Later, when she was dressing after her shower, she heard people talking outside. The guest dome was at the end of the street near the bluff. People often stood there looking at the view. She ignored the voices until a particular remark caught her attention and she became fully alert.

"It's simple," a man was saying. "It's not a cultural antiquity. It's a wreck. Therefore we're not restricted by I.P.L.'s legal codes. There is no law against salvaging a wreck on Balthor. We don't even need permits."

"There are exquisite artifacts buried in the mud in some of those rooms," said a woman. "Museums or private collectors would pay a fortune for them."

"When that computer charges and we can open the sealed hatches, who knows what we'll find inside?" a second man said.

"We'd have to get the lumpies to open the doors. I don't want to be fried like those tolats."

"What if the lumpies won't cooperate?" said the woman.

"They will," said the first man. "They scare easy if you get 'em alone."

"There might be more money in intangibles, like data in the storage banks of the computer."

"It's yours. I'm not greedy. I'll stick to what I can carry. They were fleeing a dying world, and they had a long time to pack. You can bet they brought along the best stuff they owned."

Lian moved to where she could see out the window without being seen. There were four people outside, all pretending great interest in the view of the sunset. The one who had said he wasn't greedy was the photographer, Vincent. She knew the others only by sight.

"Farr won't like it," said the woman. "Neither will the octopus."

"Old Klat? Who knows what bulbheads think? Who cares?"

"I do if he has me arrested."

"People have stolen things from every archaeological find since time began."

"Yes," agreed the other man, "but they didn't have to smuggle it light years home. They were already on Earth."

"Is it worth our reputations?" said the woman. "If we're caught—"

"It's not theft if it's a salvage job," Vincent insisted. "Besides, we won't be caught if we're smart. Nobody knows what's there, so how can they tell if anything's missing? All we have to do is high-grade the artifacts before I photo-record. What do you say?"

"Sounds good."

"But suppose the lumpies object? Try to stop us?"

"Those dummies? Forget it."

"But suppose they do? They may want what's in there."

"What could they do—cry? Besides, they haven't found any use for the stuff. It's just wasted on them."

The smallest man laughed. "That's funny," he said. "That's what the invading Europeans said about the American Indians, what Pizarro said about the Incas—why waste all that good stuff on savages?"

Vincent didn't laugh. "You're overeducated, Professor. I don't know who you're talking about, but whoever they were, they were right. Why should we let good stuff go to waste if we can get rich from it? You're older than Farr, you have more degrees than Klat, yet you're taking orders from both of them."

"I came for the experience. The honor—"

"You're a loser."

The woman intervened. "Come on, don't name-call," she pleaded. "We're all hungry, and our nerves are on edge. Let's go eat. Let's be civilized."

"Oh, we are," said the little professor with a bitter laugh. "We are."

"Suppose the lumpies tell that girl?"

"Tell her how? They can't talk." That was the last thing Lian heard as they moved off down the path.

Her first reaction was indignation and anger. How dare they! And what had that photographer done to her lumpies to make them cry? He must have done something; otherwise he wouldn't know they cried. She would tell Dr. Farr as soon as she got dressed and . . .

"Be realistic, Lian," her common sense told her. "If anyone wants to steal, they're going to. Dr. Farr can't watch them all. And this will just make him suspect everyone. There has to be a better way. The lumpies must learn to take care of themselves, like it or not."

She was late for dinner, and the dining room was crowded. As she stood in line at the autoserver, she could hear a dozen conversations, all discussing the starship. "Every dig I've been on," a man said, "the people who created the culture were dead. It's too bad this place isn't like that—it would make things a lot simpler."

"Maybe it could still be arranged?" quipped another, and there was easy laughter that gave Lian a sick feeling as she glanced at the faces around her. Someone rapped for attention, and Dr. Farr rose to speak. Lian took her food tray and sat down at the nearest table.

"I have several announcements to make," Dr. Farr began. "First, you will be happy to hear our two injured colleagues are now recovering. Tsri Zahr will return to camp in the morning.

"Now, I know you're all concerned about the current status of the expedition. Instead of a typical ruin, we have a starship that may be a colonial habitation still in use by descendants of the colonists. The ethical question arises—what right have we to trespass?

"Klat, Tsri Zahr, and I discussed the situation with the Governor General of Balthor this afternoon. We requested that this area be designated a colonial protectorate and the inhabitants be designated colonials. Our request was granted. Until we know more about the true nature of the lumpies, there will be no official announcement. We don't want visitors. Our status remains unchanged. We will proceed as normal. Except, of course, that until it is determined otherwise, all artifacts are the property of the colonials. Objects will be removed from the site only for the purpose of cleaning and identifying." He paused and scanned the room. "Are there any questions?"

"Yes." The little professor stood up, red-faced to the top of his bald head. "How dare you make such a decision without consulting the rest of us? Don't our reputations and opinions count?" Several people applauded. The man was shaking; Lian couldn't tell if it was from true anger or the need to show Vincent that he wasn't a loser.

"No," Dr. Farr said bluntly. "This is an expedition, not a democracy. Our triumvirate is responsible for the expedition's actions as a unit. Should you as individuals disagree, I refer you to the contract you signed on joining the project."

The photographer called out, "I'm here to photo-record what the rest of you dig up. But what does this ruling make you and your staff —a bunch of glorified cleaning people?"

There was an angry murmur. The man had either touched a sore point or insulted many of those present.

Farr used his cup as a gavel. "In a sense archaeologists have always been that. We can give a fair picture of a civilization by analyzing its garbage dumps. We can reconstruct a man if we find a few of his bones. Potsherds reveal magnetic polarity as well as art form. Jewelry tells us of metalworking ability, of trade and wealth and travel.

"Admittedly, this dig is different—and far more exciting. Instead of total ruin we have found, in nucleus, a new life form, a working computer to tell us the history of this species, a civilization, a world, and a star system we never knew existed. Cleaning, as you put it, is a small price to pay for such a wealth of knowledge."

"And that's all we'll take back—knowledge?"

"I hope not, but if that is all we have the right to take, it should be more than enough."

Vincent smiled a too sincere smile. "Your altruism is hard to believe," he said.

"Perhaps our ideas of what constitutes wealth differ," said Dr. Farr.

"Your documentary should sell," the little professor said quickly, as if to cover the sarcasm in the photographer's remarks and mollify Dr. Farr. "There's enough material here for volumes."

At that, conversation broke out on planned books and papers. Egos and ambitions began to surface. No real mention was made of the lumpies other than as an inconvenience or perhaps a means to an end. As she listened, Lian realized these people were, in their own way, as self-centered as her parents. They differed only in that they lacked her parents' authority, ability, and character. The exceptions were Klat and Dr. Farr and Scotty, who seemed to be genuine scholars—and the tolats.

"Details, details. Who cares?" Lian's translator picked up the voice of a tolat hissing to a companion. She grinned to herself, half agreeing. The tolats were a pragmatic crew with no thought of self-aggrandizement. She imagined their minds as neat files of schematics, thought disciplined to linear simplicity, minds that did not dance but enjoyed a game called "Jump!" Why was it that she was beginning to like them?

As soon as she was through eating, she slipped her tray and utensils into the autocleaner and went out. The streetlights turned the camp into an island of light in endless miles of wilderness. Wherever she looked around the camp's perimeter, she could see eyes gleaming back at her. They belonged to forest creatures, attracted to this artificial glow, curious and half afraid.

"Be careful," she called out to them. "Here's where the wild things are."

· 21 ·

In the stillness of the dome, four side panels opened, their runners gritting over dusty tracks. From two of these spaces emerged blue egg-shaped autocleaners. Around and around the dome they circled, leaving in their wake a width of polished floor. Vent fans kicked on, then off, while other automatic units cleaned the filters, then on again. By nightfall the dome had been made spotless, the air cool and dry.

When the Counter ceased cleaning operations in order to conserve energy, it had sanitized the dome and teaching theater. It then took visual inventory of all compartments where equipment still functioned. It saw that damage and deterioration were as bad as it had projected. Worse, the Counter was not equipped to dispose of the tons of foreign debris encrusting the main halls and hatchways.

The Counter viewed the section where the people had once lived. It had not looked in there for two generations past when the hatches sealed. The walls still glowed, but no light danced. The rooms were empty, the fountains dry, the gardens dead. The people now slept, not in their homes, but in a meditation room on the floor. Not each free and alone, but all together, these few, clustered for warmth on the cushioned pad. For lack of energy, most of what had been beautiful was gone or ruined.

The Guardian must see this. The Guardian's mind fought back; it did not sigh and resign itself to destruction. It would teach the people what the Counter could not, or so the Counter hoped.

From habit, before resting, the Counter monitored its power. For a fraction of a second (which for this unit represented a long pause), the mind was stunned by shock. The storage cells showed nineteen percent of capacity; they had shown minus one. The Counter checked and rechecked. Nothing was malfunctioning. The storage cells *had* recharged and were, in fact, still charging now from starlight. Something had cleaned a mainline luminoid!

The Counter considered this; the dormant portion of its mind might desiccate with a too-sudden power surge. Slowly, very slowly, it began to feed. But just enough, so it could think as it once could, the Counter told itself. Beneath the blue floor osmotic current crept, roiling, stimulating memories—it was intoxicating!

At three a.m. the dome lit up, an emerald glowing in the dark. It winked just once and then went out—and the Counter sobered up.

· 22 ·

Morning was dull gray. Heavy clouds hid the mountains. Lian was wakened by wortles fighting outside her door. She got up feeling grumpy. The shower water was cold, and that did not improve her mood. The only person she met on her way to breakfast was Vincent, who smiled and said, "Good morning. Looks like rain," as he fell into step beside her.

Lian had no gift for chitchat. "You and your friends leave the lumpies alone."

For an instant his smile faded, his expression went blank and then took on an adult's superior, puzzled amusement. "I don't know what your problem is, kid," he said, "and I don't want to know. Just don't bother me with it. I don't have the time." She watched him cross the grass and enter the equipment dome.

A wortle stood forlorn in the middle of the street. "Lost the fight, didn't you?" Lian commented in passing. The bird gave her an angry glare and ruffled its feathers. It looked so much the way she felt that she laughed and immediately felt better. Any world with wortles in it could not be all bad.

It was so early there were only three tolats in the dining hall. Ruby lights glowed on the beverage machines. The air smelled of hot food.

She pressed two buttons on the autoserver. Twenty-six seconds later a tray burped up, containing a yellow blob of scrambled eggs, two toasts, and a smear of grape gel. Lian looked at the food and grimaced.

"Gray people returned Zorn's recorder," a tolat announced as she sat down.

"Who's Zorn?" she said, startled that a tolat would talk in the morning.

"This tolat," said the speaker, and then she noticed its distinctive spots.

"Was the recorder O.K.? I mean undamaged?"

"Yes." Zorn pointed toward the west window. "Your three gray people are sitting."

The lumpies were huddled on the grass by the edge of the landing pad. They looked uneasy, as if they expected to be yelled at or chased at any moment. She was surprised to see them there; of all the lumpies only Billy came into the camp when he brought the beetles for Buford.

As the tolat watched, apparently fascinated, Lian made a sandwich of her food, tossed the tray into the autocleaner, mumbled, "Thank you, Zorn," and ran outside, still chewing. When they saw her, the lumpies got to their feet, all relieved smiles and finger wavings. "What are you doing here so early?"

For a moment she thought Cuddles was going to speak again. But either habit or fear was still too strong, because after a glance at the camp, Cuddles shook his head, and pointed in the direction of the site.

The four of them set off down the red dirt road. The lumpies seemed to be in a hurry and padded along on all fours. Lian had to run to keep up. "Is this necessary?" she panted after the first half mile and stopped to catch her breath. "Is anything wrong?" They smiled at her again, and from sheer frustration part of her bad mood reappeared. "You can talk! I know you can talk. Has anyone tried to hurt you?"

The three exchanged glances, and then Poonie pointed to his right side. Lian saw a round spot of what looked like blue-green ink. "What is that?" Poonie touched the spot on Lian's arm where the computer had taken samples. "The black hole pulled you in?" Then, seeing the other two were similarly wounded, she thought she understood. As timid as they were, they must have been terrified by the experience. "All of you?" They nodded. "What were you doing in the dome so early?"

Poonie said something in three soft notes, and Lian got a mental picture of doors opening. But not normal doors. Her confusion must have shown, because Poonie repeated the image.

"Not doors . . ." she said, sounding like someone playing charades. "Not doors . . . hatches opening?" Another nod. "The power cells are charging now that some of the surface is clean and the sealed hatches work?" The nods were more vigorous. "That's wonderful! Are any of the archaeologists in the hallways?"

They shook their heads. Lian hesitated, wondering if she should go back and share this news with Dr. Farr. It was his expedition, his discovery in a way. If he hadn't come here—Cuddles caught hold of her left hand and smiled up at her, and she remembered it was the lumpies' starship. "Let's go," she said.

The halls were dark and deserted when they got there. Lian thought they were going to the dome, but her guides stopped in a nondescript area and Naldo pressed a switch she couldn't even see for grime.

The hatch responded slowly. If the sun didn't shine today, how long would power last in the auxiliary equipment? She followed them in and nervously watched the hatch close behind them.

There was light inside, faint, but enough to see that the chamber was carpeted. Floor and walls were water-stained and dirty, the carpeting worn through around the door. In the distance she could hear sounds like choir members vocalizing, warming up, repeating phrases over and over.

It was easy to follow the path used over the years, plain to see which hatches had opened after the flood. Only two. One from the main corridor into this hall; one from this hall into a dim, low-ceilinged room with a camera eye gleaming in a corner. In there were all the other lumpies, looking right at home. She stepped in hesitantly, feeling she was an intruder. The floor was cushion-soft; she knelt to touch it. It felt like old velvet, shabby but warm and smelling of wild mustard. "You sleep here?" Lian asked, and Poonie nodded.

They must have been waiting for her, because no sooner had she arrived than they all began to file out. Cuddles led the way along the dingy passage to a large bulkhead hatch and pressed the switch. A crack appeared and the door slid open into a wide peach-colored hall.

Lian stared. There was a lushness to this place, a beauty she found hard to accept. Like the anteroom, it was completely sheathed in what looked like, but was not, deep silk-velvet pile that glowed with light. She thought the tolats would know where the light came from, but until they explained away the magic, she could enjoy it. Sculpture broke the monotony of plain walls. In an alcove to the left, where the passage curved, a massive gold ball floated in unexplained suspension. To the right was an elevator bank and a wide spiral ramp leading down into darkness.

She would see the ship again many times and in far greater detail, but never again would it have the same effect on her as it did that day, that first time, when she saw only what the Counter wanted them to see.

It was a little frightening, like walking through a huge deserted palace with no windows. The ship was alien and very luxurious. It was designed for large creatures, but its basic features were familiar to Lian. She had traveled Earth's deep space cruisers. Like this ship, they were self-contained bio-structures, worlds of their own.

She did not understand how the lumpies knew where they were going. They appeared more excited than nervous, and they seemed to be hunting for something in particular or some place. She heard the question, "Eteral?" repeated over and over with each large hatch that opened. And each time they looked disappointed.

There were things, the purpose of which she could only guess, products of a technology totally alien—bizarre library stacks, enormous fermentation tanks, strange machines. She saw what she was pretty sure were squat surface vehicles, balloon wheeled, burly, utilitarian. They looked new, as did what appeared to be an amphibious craft. Beyond one massive windowed balcony yawned a black cavern, and on its floor was a shuttle ship and two egg-shaped craft. It was the ship's hangar, and she wanted to see more of it, but the lumpies hurried on. They found compartments full of tools, both crated and uncrated, large drone robots and smaller multipurpose units, all with hands like metallic anemones. All looked operable.

She watched the lumpies studying, touching, fitting their hands to tools, their bodies to furnishings. They moved from one thing to the next, like children delighted but bewildered by too many birthday gifts. But eventually, no matter how fascinating the find, she would hear one of them call a reminding "Eteral?" and they would go on.

Then, along a service hall, a hatch no one had touched snapped open as if a spring had given way. They jumped, then quickly touched to reassure each other; the place was old. There was no light inside that door. A sickeningly sweet smell oozed out into the velvet hall. The lumpies backed away, their nostrils flaring as they analyzed the scent. Light from the corridor winked off a jewel lying in the darkness. Someone moved, light changed, and other jewels winked.

"Eteral?"

There was dread in the whisper, like an unspoken prayer that the answer would remain no. But they were afraid to look. Lian pulled free of Poonie's hand and went to investigate. When she flicked on the torch, someone cried out. Then silence.

It was a lounge, more lush than most, and unlike the others, this one was not empty. On the floor and draped across the furnishings were articulated bones, skeletons, and mummified remains.

She played the light over the walls, looking for high-water marks, thinking they had drowned in here. There was no sign of flooding. No one lay near the exit. Some lay together, but not in violent poses. There was no sign of panic, no suggestion that they had died trying to escape. The large, round skulls bore no fractures. Other bones appeared sturdy, unbroken.

Without warning, the hatch banged shut with a force that shuddered through the body of the ship. For a moment Lian thought she was going to be sick with terror. It was illogical; they were dead . . . the ship was . . . She rubbed her face to touch reality, felt cold sweat on her hands, and rubbed both palms dry on her sleeves. She forced herself calmly to clip the torch back onto her belt, straighten her jacket, and take a deep breath.

She turned and saw the lumpies staring at her as if she were mad. Then Poonie could stand it no longer and grabbed her hand.

It was a rout. Lian was not sure if the fear was hers alone or if it suddenly gripped them all. But they ran, all sixty-four of them, until that room was far behind. When they finally stopped, she leaned against the wall to rest and let her heart slow down. Small lumpies sank to the floor and sat exhausted. All around was the sound of deep breathing. Then someone called out, "Eteral!" and she looked up.

Just beyond their resting place the corridor widened and sloped down to an enormous ramp. Naldo stood down there, pointing to a place beyond.

· 23 ·

They hurried through an open arch and stopped still, dwarfed by a vast twilight space half a mile long and vaulting to a solar-shuttered ceiling. For minutes no one moved, stunned by awe or disappointment or both.

It had been a garden. The grass was brown and dusty, the trees dead, the flower beds brittle stalks. Along the walls on all sides, ramps led up to balconied apartment tiers that once overlooked the central green. A breeze from somewhere brushed her hair and passed. Leaves still clinging to the trees rustled. The lumpies sniffed; the air was fresh, and they relaxed with little sighs of relief.

"They lived here during the trip out?" Her voice was an alien intrusion in this old silence.

"Eteral," Poonie said, and nodded as if that word explained it all.

From a balcony mount, a camera eye came on. Within seconds lights went on in some of the apartments. The computer was tracking them! That it could still do that impressed Lian. It also made her uneasy. How much control did it still have? Did *it* decide which hatch would open and which would not? While she was puzzling over this, the lumpies began to climb the ramps.

If she had been alone, Lian would simply have walked into the first lighted place she found open. But she saw the lumpies stop to peer at what looked like nameplates on the doors, then they called out words. In response only one or two of them would enter that door . . . as if the place had once belonged to them. But if they had never been in here—

"You have family names!" Her remark struck her as stupid, and she felt herself blushing. A nearby lumpie gave her a compassionate look; the others around her just smiled.

She saw Billy and a small lumpie cross the park and climb to where another waited to enter a glowing door. "It must be sort of like going home," she said and turned. She stood alone, her trio nowhere in sight. Everyone else was searching for his own special place, and for the first time with them, she felt left out.

She shrugged and meandered up along the ramp, looking at the spots of light, trying to imagine what this place had been like when it was alive.

Where had they gone? Had they been outdoors the day the flood rushed down the valley? Did they all drown, or were they shut out when the hatches sealed in a final unexpected exile?

There was room here for hundreds of lumpies, maybe more, she thought. Now there were sixty-three.

The moongate door of an apartment lit as she passed. She checked; there was no one else about. The door split in half and slid open. Suspicious now, she looked for one of the computer's camera eyes and found it. The door was meant for her. She walked back, ill at ease but curious. What was Eteral to her?

One glance inside and she thought of the photographer and his kind. There was so much here that they could steal. The room was spacious but cluttered with belongings. It looked as if the occupants had just stepped out and might return at any moment—until you saw the dust. She edged inside, feeling like an intruder in a stranger's home.

There was no furniture as such; floor and wall space were contoured into resting places. Anything not electronic was carpeted in the glowing stuff she'd seen throughout the ship. Sculpture and artwork delineated areas. One wall contained a viewscreen. In a ledge below the screen there was a bowl-like depression full of beautiful glass marbles.

To keep from thinking much too much, she picked a dusty red marble from the bowl and polished it. As it warmed between her fingers, it began to sing, a faint sweet song somehow off-key. A book? She put it back, knowing if she did not do so quickly she would keep it, and it was not hers. And yet it seemed to be.

Through a low arch was . . . a bathroom? It contained a sunken oval vat the size of a small swimming pool, nacre-surfaced and iridescent. The hall was plainly a photo gallery. What must have been family, friends, and pets smiled out at her from the sunshine of a world long gone. Was this what the computer wanted her to see? She studied them a long time and turned away, saddened.

These things had belonged to vital, intelligent creatures. Now all were artifacts, museum pieces to be analyzed by strangers. Their very discovery would limit their existence. That seemed wrong to her, this meddling in past lives one could never understand and only coarsen by interpretation.

In the last room everything was small. Built-in shelves held toys, small lumpie dolls, spacecraft, mounted leaves and insects, and strange stuffed toy animals. Lian stood in the doorway, imagining the child who had lived here, who had tried to bring its small world along. Suddenly it all became very personal. It was as if she were seeing her own room and all the precious possessions she couldn't leave behind.

"Did they tell *you* that you weren't ever going back?" she whispered to the child across the years, remembering, never quite forgiving the fact that no one had told her. "Did you ever quit saying, 'Let's go home now'? Or did you just whisper it inside yourself, too, when you finally figured out the truth and knew there was no hope?" And then she began to cry as a child cries, in great heartbroken sobs for which there is no comfort.

Afterward, when she could think again about that morning, about that child's room, she knew it had all in some way shifted time for her and ended her own childhood. When she entered here she had walked back into the past, her own as well as theirs, had seen it whole, unalterable, and gained understanding. By the time she could return to Earth a generation of Earth time would have passed. What she longed for would be gone. *Things* might remain, a house and garden, artifacts, but all who lived within that human past lived now only in her mind. Like the lumpies, she had to start from *now,* to keep and to use what was good from the past, and forget about the rest.

She absentmindedly searched her pockets for a tissue and blew her nose, thinking that perhaps her choice of astrophysics had been her way of becoming a lumpie—of pretending to be what she was not in order to avoid—

There was a muffled thumping, and she started from her thoughts, then tiptoed down the hall. In the outer lounge stood Cuddles and Poonie, wide-eyed with worry. Naldo appeared in the entrance and gestured with both hands, then saw her. The relief that lit their faces was touching.

"Where were you?" each said in their language, and then everyone was smiling. The rest of the group was outside waiting, restless and eager to leave.

They walked the length of the sere and dusty garden. One by one the lights went out behind them. The smaller lumpies walked together now, detouring here and there, still curious, still excited. But the adults walked alone, reflectively. Like herself, Lian thought, they had been shaken by this place. She wondered what it was they had expected "Eteral" to be. And why?

The doorway out opened for them and automatically closed in their wake. The computer was still watching. Two passageways, another hatch, and they emerged into the hallway near the dome.

The Counter evaluated its efforts. It had provided access, atmosphere, and illumination. It had monitored its people and the Guardian. Energy draw: four percent with cells recharging. The minds had responded with interest, some historical recognition of equipment and places and the desire to learn. Enough power now existed to operate the training centers.

Considering the shock experiment: the people had reacted as expected, with unease and aversion. But, the Counter noted, the Guardian had thought of the *pleasure* the alien-with-white-fur-on-its-head would derive from seeing this tomb. It was this type of knowledge the Counter sought. There was no accounting for alien tastes.

If the Guardian's supposition was correct, perhaps the existence as well as the contents of this tomb could be used as a gift. Such a gift might serve two purposes: it would satisfy alien anatomical research curiosity without subjecting the living to danger; it would also clear out debris. The Counter had never condoned those deaths; if death had been the objective, much effort could have been spared by merely remaining on their home world.

The next move must be calculated. Note that the Guardian learned quickly and was worthy of some degree of trust. Note that its people feared humans more than other aliens. Note that the Guardian feared some humans for the people's sake. . . .

· 24 ·

Like the lumpies, Lian had had enough of enclosed spaces. She was on her way out when Scotty called from the dome. "Lian, is that you?"

"No."

"Can you come in here and listen to this? Bring your friends."

Only the trio would come with her. The others wandered away down the corridor.

Scotty, Zorn, and other tolats had set up shop to translate in the dome itself. Lian saw a folding table and a chair for Scotty, a portable terminal and other equipment.

"You're going to work in here?"

"We thought we'd try it. The lumpies never come into camp, except Billy, so we'd never hear them if they did talk," Scotty explained. "And I thought maybe playing this recording might inspire them or their computer to help us."

"Also it is raining. Roof of our workshop drips," said Zorn. "Tolats do not like wet equipment."

"No. I imagine not." Lian's mind was not quite with them as she looked up at the rain-streaked glass overhead. The sight of clouds and living trees moving in the wind outside made her feel better.

"I'm sorry," said Scotty. "Did I intrude? Were you going someplace with the group?"

"We were going out for air. We've been exploring."

"I guessed that. You're all grubby as miners. Find anything interesting?"

"Talk later," suggested Zorn. "Tsri Scott said you heard gray people speak and maybe understand. Listen." He turned on the recorder. The lumpies smiled at the sound of their own voices and sat down to listen. Lian joined them. "Can you slow it down?" she said. "As slow as possible without distortion."

"Who knows distortion?" said Zorn, but did as she asked. The voices deepened but became no more intelligible to her.

"Is that gray Cuddles' voice?"

Before Lian could answer, Cuddles smiled and nodded.

"What is gray Cuddles saying?"

"I don't know," Lian admitted. "Scotty, how long will it take you if you have to translate the hard way—word for word?"

"The hard way?" Scotty grinned. "A year, perhaps longer. I'm not sure of one printed symbol so far—"

"Display screen," Zorn interrupted. His gripper claw pointed to the Counter, where the panel was sliding open.

"Lis-son!" The hidden amplifiers boomed the sibilant word, and everybody jumped at the volume. "Lis-son!" it repeated. "I will talk and you can all smile. . . ." As it spoke, those odd, sporelike characters appeared on the screen, and Scotty's forehead furrowed in attention. "Are those words—printed words—or an image of the sound?" she wondered aloud to herself.

"It's repeating something I said—" Lian started to explain when the word, "Lis-son," boomed again. She obediently shut up.

Several tolats edged closer to the golden machine and peered at it as if searching for its mouth. The other staff members came hurrying into the dome. They were followed by lumpies and Dr. Farr, struggling to get through the sudden crush at the gate. "You're going to have to lower your speakers," the man said. "You're deafening the entire—"

"Lis-son!" the Counter repeated. "I—will—translate!" Camera eyes focused on Lian and on the crowded ramp. The volume lowered. "I—will—translate!"

Dr. Farr stopped short. A tolat had to jump over him to avoid a direct crash. The man's face went pale.

The Counter spoke in singing tones and the lumpies answered. Then Naldo held out his hand to Zorn, took the recorder, and pressed the proper buttons.

At first haltingly and then with greater confidence, the Counter translated into Lian's language and in tones oddly close to her voice the recording Cuddles had made when the trio had borrowed the recorder.

". . . I am the prime historian and retain the images, old and vivid, perspectives down remembered corridors of time. . . . We are Toapa from a world that circled Ohran."

Cuddles told of a time in flight, long before any of this generation was born. Just how long ago he could not say, but it was remembered as peaceful and safe.

"The peace ended with the landing on this world."

The Counter brought the great ship down with almost pinpoint accuracy, but even so, its bulk grazed the river and plowed across the valley. Its jets denuded and pulverized a wide strip of land between the river and the landing site. Its great mass depressed the soil and rock beneath it.

The rainy season came. Water draining from the mountains swelled the river. It overflowed at its weakest point and made a channel of that strip. A wall of rushing water, mud, and tree trunks swirled down upon them. The main hatch was open and twisted off. Water poured into the ship. Many drowned or were swept away to die.

"Illness came, and bidernecks, and despair."

Cuddles was not sure, but he thought the flood came many times in those early years.

Before the flood the people used the planet's surface as a park, a place to play, to escape the confines of the ship. They did not want to believe they would have to live out there, to take care of themselves. But they began to try because they had no choice. They planted orchards from the ship's dying gardens. They computer-analyzed and tasted plants. They learned of hunger, cold, and fear—things no amount of empathy could cure.

Mud gradually buried the ship. The Counter's power waned. It could not function properly, could not care for them. Hatches shut and remained shut for lack of power. The ship was vacated as a death trap. Only a select few had ever entered the dome. Within a generation those few were dead. The existence of the dome itself was almost forgotten. The Counter remained in the songs and oral history of its people as a sort of god that failed, through no fault of its own.

In time, said Cuddles, many of their people left the area of the ship. Other races discovered the world. His people tried to communicate with them and failed. But they could understand the aliens' thoughts. Some of them died, killed by despair. They had known they were helpless, but not that they were contemptible, that their very appearance put them beyond consideration as sentient beings. Some were shot for sport and some for their beautiful soft hides; others were shipped to zoos. Some went mad and wandered off into the wilderness.

The few who remained and were sane came back to this place. They taught themselves a sign language. They never sang again where they might be overheard, never showed any sign of feeling, any kind of thought or intelligence.

"To survive they tried to become what other aliens wanted to believe they were—fat and stupid animals."

When she heard that part, Lian began to cry. Scotty gave her a paper hankie, then on impulse gave one each to the three lumpies and used one herself. All five wiped their eyes while the tolats stared.

The recording ended. There was silence in the dome, and then scattered pockets of hushed conversation broke out. Lian sat on the floor, hugging her knees, tears still running down her face, thinking of mad lost lumpies wandering this hostile world. She was almost sure that it had been one of those who climbed up on her wrecked aircar that night. As a telepath it might have been attracted by her own fears or lonely thoughts, maybe seeking a kindred mind?

Dr. Farr came out of deep thought and cleared his throat. "How tragic—but how absolutely fascinating," he said. "How did you get the computer working? Did you find a switch?"

"No," said Zorn.

"It—uh—volunteered," said Scotty. "Like it did before."

"But how could it know our language? We can't understand a word of theirs. Correct?"

"Correct," said Scotty.

"Computer records every sound," said Zorn, and pointed. "Cameras work. Why not rest of unit?"

"Can we ask them questions?" Dr. Farr addressed this to Lian. "Can we speak to the—uh—Toapa through it?"

"We can try."

The Counter listened to this exchange and to the thoughts of the aliens as it analyzed what it had just translated. Like the aliens, the Counter was surprised—if not to the same degree. It had been unaware of all the hardships its people had faced, had not realized how unobservant it had become as it lost power. It felt new grief, and new respect for them.

Some of the aliens could not yet truly comprehend or accept the meaning of what they had heard. They now verbalized to cover lack of understanding. Other thoughts were of pity and guilt; a few were empathetic, some angry and resentful; some were very frightened. One human left the room. The Counter noted with approval the Guardian seemed least surprised of all; her mind was weaving facts together, calculating. The white-furred one was disappointed with itself because it had failed to understand and now took refuge in incidental questions of mechanics. They were, the Counter concluded, a relatively primitive lot.

It had told them—and more importantly, told the Guardian—what its people wanted known about themselves. The people had omitted much. The Counter would respect this. It might not be wise to expose the aliens to the further shock of learning, for example, just what the Counter was: the essence of the best minds of seven generations of Toapa. Some of these alien minds might try to destroy the Counter or the people out of fear, and the Counter would have to stop them. Better to remain the aliens' conception of a computer . . . to emulate a lumpie . . . .

· *25* ·

They tried, but the Counter did not answer questions. Nor would the lumpies say more. Before ten minutes had passed, some of Dr. Farr's staff recalled how much the computer's voice had sounded like Lian's. They began to wonder if they had been hoaxed. They left for lunch, discussing their suspicions as they went. The cameras watched them go.

"I'm sorry." Dr. Farr apologized for some of the less kind remarks.

Lian shrugged. "In their place I might be suspicious, too," she said, and thought how little it would take to change their attitudes. If the lumpies and their Counter wanted these people to know the rest of the ship was now accessible, they would do so. They had not, and so she would keep that secret.

"Humans are not smart," Zorn declared. "This is not machine as tolats know machines, not simple as tolats know simple"—the creature hissed and raised its rodlike eyes—"but as gray people once knew simple. . . ."

Something about Zorn's sudden interest made the three lumpies back away. The tolat turned and pointed a claw at Lian. "You said computer pulled you in?"

"Yes. The first time I came in here."

"You learned something in there?"

"Yes, but—"

Zorn did not listen but raced to the end of the computer and disappeared inside. Lian held her breath, remembering. Not quite a minute passed; there was a whisked sound, and Zorn was shot out, bowled halfway across the shiny floor.

Everybody ran to help the tolat. The crowd of lumpies stared wide-eyed, then, seeing him unharmed, exchanged glances. Their round gray stomachs began to shake, and they left the dome to hide their laughter. Only the trio stayed behind.

Still on the floor, Zorn told a fellow tolat, "You try!" The other's eyes shot straight up, and Lian imagined she could see its indignation. "No!" it said. The rest of the tolats suddenly had business elsewhere.

"I'll try," said Dr. Farr, and walked into the darkness with one hand outstretched to feel the way. His fingers buckled against a solid wall. "It's closed!" He sounded both disappointed and relieved as he patted the barrier. "I can't get in. What did you learn, Zorn?"

"This tolat felt one mind," said Zorn, "but not for long. It does not trust us. Only Tsri Lian and its own people."

"You're right," said Dr. Farr. "That's a very wise machine."

"But of us all, tolats would be the only ones who might be able to fix it if it needs repairs," said Scotty.

The Counter had already considered that. It was for that reason it had expelled the clever alien. It feared being merely chemically or mechanically understood by them, tampered with into insanity or paralysis, and then, perhaps, remade immortal. It thought the tolats might try to do that with the best of intentions, unaware of what they were destroying.

"I think we're trying to hurry things," Dr. Farr decided. "We haven't begun to consider what we've just been told, and we're looking for more. Klat, what is your opinion?"

"That we discuss things while we feed," said Klat.

Lian was not hungry, nor did she feel like listening to people. Scotty volunteered to bring her back a sandwich. When they had gone, Lian wandered over to stare at the Counter. She was sorry it would not translate. There were so many questions she wanted to ask the lumpies about the things they'd seen this morning, about their history—and what were their real names? When they could communicate totally, she thought, how was she going to explain the names she'd given them? Could she say, "I looked upon you as pets, large but good-natured and affectionate"? Then the thought occurred to her that if they were as smart as she suspected they were, they might call her the Toapa equivalent of Fido. . . .What did the word "guardian" mean to them . . . ?

She looked over and saw the three of them still sitting there, not smiling now but watching tolats trying to test the floor. Since they weren't going to hide any more, they should move out of the ship, she thought. They would need houses, water, and waste recycle systems—education. The strip of land between ship and river was good soil for gardens. Maybe she could teach them . . . .

She helped herself to one of Scotty's sketching pads and a pen. "Let's design you a home," she suggested to the trio. "We could build it on the bluff where the camp is now. There's a beautiful view—" Poonie picked up the pad and examined it minutely before giving it back to Lian with a mental question mark.

"Paper. To draw and write on. See." Lian began to sketch the kind of house she would like to live in, the kind of house she remembered. As she drew, the trio watched and whispered to one another. When she had finished, Cuddles reached for the pen. He made a few awkward experimental strokes; then Poonie took the pen and turned to a fresh page.

Soon all four of them were stretched on the warm floor, engrossed in house design, oblivious to all around them. Raindrops beaded on the roof overhead, flattened, and made rivulets down the glass. The dome was quiet except for the click of tolat claws and the murmur of voices in the corridor outside.

The house Poonie drew somehow looked like the gray people. It was large and nicely rounded with a garden and a moongate. It stood by itself on the side of a wooded hill.

"Where does everybody else live?" said Lian.

Cuddles got up and padded over to the table and got another pen. He and Naldo collaborated on a village. Their drawing, like Poonie's, had a sense of humor to it, Lian thought. Small furry things like Buford were given a guest house. Allowance was made to avoid wortle burrows and paths in the cliff above the river.

A passing tolat stopped to study the sketch. "Nice," it decided. "But fountain should be here." A claw pointed. "Here we can bring waterfall down to pool in center. Stream can recycle down to river."

"Can we make the pool deep enough for them to swim?"

"Tolats can do anything if they have right tools," said the tolat, and elbowed in to join the party.

Dr. Farr and Scotty wandered in and stood over them. The group worked on, unaware of their audience until Lian said, "Somebody's blocking the light," and looked up to see the two staring openmouthed at the sketches.

"They drew that?" Dr. Farr whispered, as if he didn't want to break a spell. Lian nodded. "So they *do* retain images from the past. . . . I wondered what that line meant. As telepaths they can pass along from generation to generation how things truly were. Oral historians were quite common among Earth's tribes, but to find a culture like this!" For a moment he looked as if he'd like to shout for joy, and then he visibly regained self-control. "Yes, well . . . are the towers an abstract fountain?"

"That's the waste recycle system," Lian explained. "The tolats are going to build it. Look at the foliage on the trees. It's not leaves; it looks like tiny script. And there, see a pattern on the cliff road? It's more notes." At that Scotty went over to get her note pad and joined them.

Dr. Farr put on his glasses and knelt down. "Amazing!"

"That they can write?"

"At this point that doesn't surprise me at all," he said. "Perhaps it would if I thought about it. What amazes me is that I missed the advance of several centuries by going to lunch."

A commotion broke out in the corridor. Faint shouting could be heard, then running footsteps.

"Dr. Farr? Dr. Farr?" The man Lian thought of as the little professor came running down the ramp into the dome. He was soaking wet, and his face was sickly pale. She sat up, alarmed before he spoke. "Dr. Farr! You've got to come!" He was panting with exertion. "You too, miss. They trust you. Hurry! They might kill him!"

Lian was up and running, the lumpies ahead of her. The corridor had never seemed so long. She dodged the curious staffers, never heard them speak. What had that stupid person done to make her gentle lumpies threaten him? Behind her she could hear the others coming, Scotty calling for her to wait.

Outside she paused. No one was in sight. It was raining hard. The three lumpies never hesitated but scrambled up over the earthwork, their feet slipping in the wet ground and leaves. She took a great gulp of fresh, sweet air and followed them. She didn't have far to go.

On the opposite side of the earthwork, in the hollow of a fallen tree, stood Vincent, his back against the roots. He was encircled by lumpies. They stood shoulder to shoulder, hands folded on their chests, watching him. He looked terrified.

"Call them off!" he yelled when he saw Lian.

"Coward," she said. "What's under your jacket?"

He glanced down and tried to flatten the bulges around his middle. Failing, he shoved his hands into his pockets.

"What did you steal?"

"Nothing! Just get them away from me!"

Cuddles called something, and all the lumpies stood erect. Vincent took one look, turned, and tried to scramble up over the tangled roots of the stump. A tall lumpie caught him by the armpits, lifted him up and held him like a flailing insect, then gave him a vigorous shake. It was a very impressive display of strength.

"Stop! You're crazy!" Vincent got another shaking. "Stop it! It'll break! Stop!" There was a flash of color. Objects began to fall from the man's clothing into the mud below, and the lumpies retrieved them. A final shake and a small oblong panel fell. The lumpie turned and put him down outside their circle. He ran in panic, straight into Dr. Farr at the top of the slope.

"You've got to take some security measures, Farr!" The man grasped the archaeologist's arms to keep from falling. "Those animals tried to kill me! Look at this!" He showed them the dirt on his clothes. Dr. Farr was not impressed. Without commenting, he freed himself and came down to where Lian and the lumpies stood.

"Is that what was taken?" he asked Lian, looking at the enamel picture of a flower from a lost planet, a jeweled armpiece, an engraved something, and two drinking bowls held by the lumpies. "Beautiful!"

"I was only going to photograph the stuff," said Vincent. "I wasn't going to take it. I was . . ."

Dr. Farr looked at him now for the first time. "Of course you were," he said mildly.

Vincent flushed. "I get attacked and you get sarcastic."

"You weren't attacked—you were caught," said Lian. "They didn't hurt you. They just took back what was theirs."

There was finger talking among the lumpies, and then those holding the objects in question stepped forward and held them out to Dr. Farr. "For safekeeping? Surely—" There was more rapid discussion and then head shaking.

"Gifts?" Lian was guessing. The lumpies nodded.

The photographer said a nasty word. "If they don't want it anyhow, what difference did it make if I had it?"

"Some of us are particular about who we want to own our things," said Lian, and Scotty laughed.

Dr. Farr did not. "I'm sure you were rather discreet, handling such beautiful items, especially since none of us had yet seen them," he said to Vincent. "Yet the—uh—Toapa knew you had them. If I were you, I'd think about that. This could be an object lesson."

Vincent was going to protest, but then he saw Lian and the lumpies looking at him. He swore again and walked off through the rain.

"Are you going to dismiss him?" the professor asked nervously.

"No. Without Earth passage booked he'd be stranded in Limai for months. Talking too much. He's a very good photographer . . . and I want him where we can keep an eye on him."

26

That evening, like the good host he was, and in spite of the rain, Dr. Farr joined Lian beneath her tree to stand and watch twilight come over the mountains. The lumpies were swimming in the river below, but for the first time none of the staff had gone down to watch them.

"Why do you suppose that is?" she asked when he commented on that fact.

"Because of you," he said when she had almost given up hope of getting an answer. "Like the serpent in the garden, you've made us aware. Before you came we saw them as animals, innocents. Now they are sentient—with a past and dignity and a name. Long ago there was great magic in names. It was believed you could be destroyed by anyone who knew your true name. They were sacred words of great power. . . ."

Lian shivered. "Do you believe that?" she asked.

"That's superstition. Ages ago, worlds past."

"But was it true?"

"There is some truth in most myths."

"My mother said lost tribes seldom survive discovery."

"And you're afraid that sort of thing will happen here?"

"Aren't you?"

"It had occurred to me," he admitted.

"If I'd never come here, maybe—"

"Don't assume too much responsibility, Lian," he said quickly. "Granted, discovery represents risk for them. But to avoid it, all they had to do was hide. There is more than enough room to hide on Balthor.

"My theory is they knew time was running short—that if they hid and continued to play stupid for another generation, they might truly become so—or they might die out. I suspect they chose to take the risk of exploitation or death rather than to continue to deny their intelligence."

Or the Counter chose to, thought Lian, but why through me?

"In any event," Dr. Farr continued, "we have discovered them. That can't be changed. If their things are all of beauty equal to those gifts they gave us today, then there is great wealth here. Wealth attracts greed. I will do what I can to protect them. So will Klat and his people. And the tolats will protect that engineering marvel in the dome until they understand it. For that they need its owners—and so they will protect them. But a lot of their future will depend on the lumpies— and perhaps on you, if you choose to accept it. They trust you. I don't pretend to have a theory as to why—or perhaps there is no *why* but only circumstances."

"Listen," said Lian, who was not quite ready to consider the responsibility implied by the man's last remark.

Unlike other evenings, the swimmers in the river had begun to call to one another, their voices floating rich and clear in the still air. As if hearing the sounds inspired confidence, the phrases grew louder, more elaborate, and the hills gave back an echo. From downriver a voice sang out and another answered. The first repeated and then joined the second. Two more joined in, repeating the same phrase.

"They're singing!" There was wonder in his voice.

"Shhh!"

"Can you understand the words?"

"No," she whispered. "Just listen." There were voices in the camp behind them, and she turned to see the staff gathering, shushing one another, curious to hear. A tolat was jumping to the equipment shed, probably to get a recorder. She wondered what they would make of this music in translation.

The song was short and happy. It no sooner ended than another began; more voices joined in. Across the water by the shell beds, Poonie stood waist high in the river and began to sing. The others fell silent to listen. Poonie's voice was high and sweet, and the song was haunting. Then at intervals, individually or in chorus, other voices joined in.

Lian heard the music as a tale of good and evil, in times long past with people long gone, sung now not for its moral but for its beauty and their joy in at last being free to sing again.

The clouds broke, the wind shifted, and one by one the stars glittered. Still the music drifted across the water and traced memories in listening minds.

When it was almost night, the lumpies left the river and gathered on the beach. All in a company, they melted into the darkness of the forest, their voices echoing back and back again from the wet hills.

With the singing ended, the staff headed toward the dining room. Soon the only sounds were forest noises and a burr of distant conversation. Lian and Dr. Farr still stood leaning against the tree, each lost in private thoughts. Then with a sigh the man said, "I guess we should go eat."

"I guess so."

"I expect we'll hear from your parents soon."

"Either that or they'll just send Max to pick me up."

"Are you sure you want to go back?" And then to soften the bluntness of his question, "Being here seems to agree with you. Like the lumpies, your expression is changing, your face is becoming more open. You're not quite the same too-serious young person you were the day we met."

"That seems like a long, long time ago," Lian said, and smiled. "I don't want to go back, to be honest. I'm not even sure now if I want to be an astrophysicist. I want to stay here—so much that it feels wrong even to think about being anywhere else. I know this might not be a forever thing—like a career—but maybe . . . maybe I could become the leading expert on the Toapa? Would you mind?"

"I'd be very glad—and so would Scotty and your tolat friends. You can help with the translation problem and act as liaison . . ." By the camp lights she saw him frown. "But I think you'd better call the observatory. Your parents might not approve at all."

"Not at first," she agreed, "but when they understand what it is we've found here, they will."

"Are you sure?"

"Not positive. But I think so. They're very intelligent," she said, and wondered why Dr. Farr began to smile and then controlled the urge.

"Perhaps so," he said, "but I have visions of an irate visit from them."

"Never irate. Never a scene," she said. "They aren't like that at all."

"What are they like, Lian? I'm curious."

She looked up at the supernova, thinking over her answer. "They are bright, rather remote—absentminded people. They enjoy their work so much that I don't think it has ever occurred to them that it is work. To them it's fun. They care very much for each other; they are friends and collaborators. They've spent so many years looking into deep space . . . that their sense of perspective is different. They seldom see what's going on around them.

"I remember once my mother was holding my hand before I went back to sleep after a bad dream, and to comfort me she said, 'There in your small finger is an iron atom born in the death of a star. It passed through the gaseous clouds of space, whirled into and out of Earth's sun to Earth, passed through mountains and prehistoric seas, dinosaurs, a fish and a fisherman, the north wind, a rabbit, a river and steel and rust. It is immortal. We are all immortal atoms.' "

"And were you comforted?" Dr. Farr said gently when she fell silent.

"In an odd way, yes. Because she meant it to comfort. She is not a once-upon-a-time person . . . my small left finger has always seemed very special to me. I used to look at it under a microscope to see if I could find that immortal atom . . . now I know it will always be there, whether I see it or not."

27

When all the little minds warped into sleep, the Counter ceased to monitor. It seldom listened in on dreams, not from discretion, but because the dream content of mortals was often painful, reminding some of its component parts of past dreams of their own—before they became the Counter and were trapped forever in this form. For the Counter, no dream was a sweet dream.

Throughout the night it occupied itself with work. Lessons were sorted through and selected. The adults would first learn practical skills; the young could begin at the beginning. Care must be taken to avoid rousing alien fears of the unknown. A theater within the still-private section of the ship was readied as a classroom.

Here and there within the system, machine repaired machine. Robot arms jerked to life. Scanning eyes lit up. Drone arms pulled rover units into charge. Cleaner units rolled to maintenance and tidied up the ship. Squeaking like bats in the dark, three rover units traveled down the ramps to the deep holds. There they located equipment, silicon converters, molders, extruders. The people would need this soon. At long last the people were planning to build!

They would need surveyors and drafters and diggers. And where was that foaming machine? All the work could be done by drone robots and

—the Counter came to a halt. It was doing it again—planning to take total care of its people. It remembered how that had worked out before. It would not make that mistake again.

The Counter had opened up the ship, and the people would not enter until they could share it with the Guardian—who seemed as much at home in their ship as they did. The Guardian sketched a crude outline of a house and with it set Toapa minds to dancing, and because of that they planned to build.

The Counter considered the over-all results of its testing and analyses of the sixty-three that morning. These people were not like the landing generation. During the years of the Counter's quiescence, they had become an altered strain. Toapa still, but made different by a new world. Like the Guardian, they were survivors. They planned to go on.

At the lowest point in its life, the Counter had chosen the Guardian. Looking back on that now, with twenty-nine percent energy capacity, the Counter thought perhaps that had been an act of desperation. But no mistake. The form was alien but the mind was somehow akin. Like the Counter and its people, the Guardian had lived in isolation and imposed innocence, enduring the present by memories of a secure past. And survived almost whole. Between Guardian and people there was now a common bond, although none knew it but the Counter. They would grow up together.

The Counter would watch and provide, not as much as it possibly could—but only as much as was good for its people, enough to allow them to become independent and self-sustaining and whole.

When these sixty-three were established, perhaps it could call in the others, the lost and wild ones, make them sane again. Considering the greed of some aliens and the indignities suffered from others, and projecting over the months ahead, there would be a need for defense. Rover units could be disguised as rocks and placed at strategic points around the site. The Counter had never had to consider defense against living creatures; it was unsure what measures were needed. Possibly it had something to do with anger—although that seemed very inefficient. Prevention, more likely. There was so much to learn!

The pure mind that was the Counter considered the implications of that thought.

For the first time in three hundred years it sang to itself in the darkness